MRS. HENSWORTHY'S BOOKCASE³
FORBIDDEN FRUIT

*Another Tale of Science Fiction, Served with
Tea and Biscuits*

By

Norman J Barta

BALINOR BOOKS
2024

Enjoy these other fine works from Balinor Books, now available at Amazon.com!

The Continuing Adventures of Sir Roderick Melrose
A titillating erotic romance and humorous travel adventure in the Victorian vernacular

The Conversational Poet
Love, wit and wisdom celebrated in the joy of verse

A Little Jaunt through Scandinavia,
or Norman and Lisa's Nordic Adventure in The Year of Our Volvo 2001

Mrs. Hensworthy's Bookcase
A Tale of Science Fiction, Served with Tea and Biscuits

Mrs. Hensworthy's Bookcase^2
Interdimensional Commerce

About the author:

Norman J. Barta was born on an unassuming little planet circling a fairly ordinary little star residing in an arm of a fairly ordinary little galaxy; it's not even the first planet in its star system, but, of all things, the *third* planet. He tries not to dwell on this fact, as the first and second planets really aren't very hospitable anyway.

He tells his fellow planetary occupants that he's 134 years old; people inevitably respond with, "Oh, but you look so young!" If he told them his true age, they'd probably just say, "That's nice, dear."

He aspires to the title of "Renaissance Person." Vocationally, he's an entrepreneur working on exciting device-driven changes in medical care. Avocationally, he's a modest and unassuming author, poet, architect, artist, cabinet-maker and musician.

www.njbarta.com provides a peek at some of the pursuits that float his proverbial boat (although we might mention that boating is not necessarily one of those pursuits). Please enjoy the journey through his writings!

MRS. HENSWORTHY'S BOOKCASE[3]
FORBIDDEN FRUIT

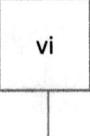

1

Brobding Measelfort was deep in thought.

As you may recall, Brobding was from the planet Measel, and, in contrast to his most congenial personality, rather resembled a large 16-legged bedbug. And as I'm sure I have no need to remind you (but will do so anyway), Brobding worked for the MITE Corporation, as one of the skilled workers who maintained the transdimensional transport tubes that kept commerce buzzing in the nearby galactic neighborhood. But back to our story.

Brobding had been trying to figure out a side business in which he might engage; he was getting a bit bored of the transdimensional transport tube repair business, and was also somewhat motivated to improve his income. His overbearing aunt on his mother's side, Measelanna Hooscod, kept trying to introduce him to suitable Measeloot mates (which is, by the way, how one refers to those from the planet Measel; Measeloot, that is, not mates), and he thought he might be more comfortable with the idea of a relationship if he was better able to pay for things; he had been told by several Measeloot associates that dating could be, in fact, quite expensive.

As for Brobding's earlier escapades on the subject of a side business, he didn't have much luck trying to import tea from Barnork 3 (or, as you probably refer to it, Earth) to certain of the planets in the local Trading League. Just in case it slipped your mind, the tea he imported had some rather extraordinary effects on the indigenous populations. The most notable of these effects was the vast growth of fluffy pink fur on the inhabitants of the Kor Planets. While this may have been quite useful from the perspective of the pink fur coat manufacturers, and certainly helped to keep the Korpits warm in the wintertime, it had presented certain extraordinary challenges to those trying to see through all the fur on their appendages. There had been numerous incidents of Korpits rolling over one another. It was not pretty. All in all, not the most successful venture.

At any given moment, Brobding was devoting at least 36.738% of his left brain to the problem at hand. And one day, while working on a particularly tedious tube repair once again involving the presence of Sleebortikan slime, a thought made itself known. Unfortunately, the Sleebortikan slime residue was giving Brobding more trouble than usual, so the thought was delayed approximately 47.344 minutes, for those using Barnorklet time parameters, until Brobding had managed to vacuum up all of the residue powder which is typically associated with the cleaning of Sleebortikan slime.

As for the thought, Brobding recalled that his associate on the tea venture, Dearlotin Farpelmop, or, as his cohorts referred to him, 'Farpel,' was in the process of distributing a variety of products throughout the Trading League; Farpel was rather a nefarious character, who tended to think of the planetary and galactic laws primarily as suggestions, but he had a knack for moving products around. Perhaps he would have an interesting product opportunity for Brobding to pursue.

If we may digress for a moment, please remember that, before he turned to a life of questionable and/or hedonistic pursuits, Dearlotin Farpelmop was a star student of Lorkin Lort, renowned Professor of Multidimensional Physics at Lechien 7's Center for Education in the Galactic Sciences. Professor Lort was one of the key figures in mapping the interdimensional folds that formed the very foundation of the transdimensional transport network. This of course brought to life the MITE Corporation, which maintains the current network of transdimensional transport tubes, and allowed commerce to move from one planet to another with essentially the same ease as travelers had earlier enjoyed in moving from town to town on their own planets.

Under Professor Lort's tutelage, Farpel learned all about interdimensional folds. His education went well past the theoretical, however, as he delved into the practical aspects of addressing both different subsets of n-space, and the functionality of interdimensional folding within those subsets. This had proven extremely useful in what one might refer to as 'underground commerce,' as Farpel opened an interdimensional rift in one location to retrieve goods into a particular 3-space of his choosing, and shifted the goods through a similar rift in another location to deliver them. But let's continue.

Brobding hadn't been in direct contact with Farpel for quite some time; he heard that Farpel had been vacationing on Wowserlik 3, a planet renowned throughout this particular galactic neighborhood for its spectacular beaches, but that was a while ago now.

Brobding decided to contact his favorite cousin, Willodig Propmeasel, a restaurateur and caterer on their home planet of Measel. Willodig was the one who had first introduced Brobding to Farpel, so Brobding thought that perhaps Willodig would know his whereabouts.

Picking up his Holo-CalloMatic with his appendage number 3 (that would be more or less central to his left side), Brobding tried to connect with his cousin. As you recall, the Holo-CalloMatic allowed conversations that included holographic projections of the participants.

In short order, he saw a projection of Willodig appear before him. Willodig was addressing someone out of Brobding's line of sight as he tasted some purplish concoction with funny-looking yellow balls floating about in the brew. "Garvo, this is going to need a lot more mashed zekkehweed if it's going to satisfy that party from Walinga 5. Oh, emoclew, Brobding; what do you want? As you can see, I'm up to my schlorkins in Zekkeh Stew."

I'm sure you remember that 'emoclew' is one of the more popular terms of greeting on planet Measel, and, when spelled phonetically, just happens to be the Earth term 'welcome' spelled backwards. A truly remarkable coincidence.

"Emoclew, Willodig, and I'm fine, thanks for asking. Since you want me to get straight to the point, I wanted to know if you've had any contact with Farpel recently."

Willodig stared at the Zekkeh Stew, mixing it slowly and carefully as he considered the question. "No, cousin, I frankly haven't had any interaction with that Farpel fellow since that business with the druzhia....uh, tea. I can try to reach him through channels, but it will be a few planetary rotations; I just have too many parties going on. I'm sure you're aware that it's graduation time throughout the Trading League planets, and everybody and his bortle is having a celebratory shindig."

"You know, I seem to recall that friend of yours, what was her name again, Kolameas Elwinkem? I heard through the polanka vine that she's had some interaction with Farpel. You could try contacting her; maybe she knows where he is."

Brobding shuddered involuntarily. Kolameas Elwinkem was a rather annoying and somewhat vacuous Measeloot who had shown *far* too much interest in Brobding for his particular taste; the thought of actually proactively contacting her gave him a notable case of indigestion. "Well, I'm not in that much of a hurry; if it's all the same to you, I'd rather wait for you to try finding him."

Several days later, at least from the perspective of a Measeloot, Brobding's Holo-CalloMatic vibrated; it was Willodig.

"Emoclew, Willodig; how goes the party circuit?"

Willodig was busy plucking some sort of horns from a dish set before him. He continued to pluck as he spoke to Brobding. "Emoclew, Brobding; this smoked gridnap was *supposed* to be dehorned *before* it left the kitchen, so now, of course, I'm left to do the job myself. It's getting to the point where it's not even worth serving this stuff."

"In any case, I just wanted to let you know that I reached out through channels to your friend Farpel, and was told that he'll be contacting you shortly." He suddenly turned to a server coming out of the kitchen. "No, no, no! Wait a minute, you can't serve those roasted whartikins without the kaportled cream! Brobding, I really need to go!" And with that, Willodig signed off abruptly.

'Well, that was a little rude,' thought Brobding, as he returned to his tube work, but as a Measeloot, it was pretty much impossible for him to dwell on a negative emotion for any significant length of time.

The very next evening, Brobding had just wrapped up his work for the day when his Holo-CalloMatic vibrated again; he opened the projection, and saw Dearlotin Farpelmop before him, with what appeared to be a large expanse of beach behind him. As you know, Farpel was a Kinglorf, specifically from Kingl 5, and, for those acquainted with various Earth species, looked pretty much like a Great Dane, but with four extra appendages. At the moment, he happened to be wearing a funny-looking hat. And if you can picture a Great Dane wearing a funny-looking hat, it's reasonably amusing.

Much to Brobding's surprise, Kolameas Elwinkem poked herself into the projection, and was the first to address him.

"Hi, Brobding! It's me! Kolameas! Kolameas Elwinkem! I'm here at the beach with Farpel and we're having such fun! Are you having fun? I hope you're having fun! Oh, look, there's more sand over there! Well, bye!" At that moment, Farpel was in the process of moving so that Kolameas was now out of view, and proceeded to address Brobding himself.

"Greetings, Meas! How's life in your particular 3-space? I heard through the polanka vine that you were looking for me." Farpel stood with a large beverage held in one appendage, sucking up the brilliant orange contents with two straws, while holding some seemingly edible concoction with another appendage. "What's up?"

Brobding took a moment to recover from his encounter with Kolameas before he could muster a response. "Uh, emoclew, or rather, hi, Farpel. I was just a little surprised to see Kolameas Elwinkem in your company."

"Yeah, nothing too serious there," Farpel murmured in a low tone. Brobding watched as Farpel seemed to move further away from his earlier position. Farpel then spoke in almost a whisper. "Truth be known, Meas, she's driving me a little *nuts*. By next week, I plan to find a quiet place to create an interdimensional rift, and slip into a different 3-space. There's only so much Elwinkem one guy can take."

Brobding understood all too well the issue at hand, even though he didn't necessarily approve of Farpel's rather abrupt plan of action. "Well, Farpel, do try to be diplomatic about it; Kolameas can be REALLY annoying, but she has good intentions."

"Got it, Meas; you know me, Mr. Smooth. Now what's up? I got a meeting with one of my gambling 'employees' coming up." While continuing to balance drink and sustenance, Farpel added definitive quotes using his two additional appendages.

"Well, I would like to pursue another product distribution opportunity, and thought perhaps you might have some thoughts on the subject. I know we can count on Mrs. Hensworthy to help us if we have any involvement with Barnork 3."

Farpel wore a noticeable smile. "You know, it's funny you should mention that. I was just thinking about a possibility for that planet. You probably know that I distribute Biepal throughout the Trading League. You know the Barnorklets better than I do; what do you think? Is there a Biepal market there?"

To clarify for those not acquainted with the substance, Biepal is an intoxicating beverage derived from the juice of the biepalfruit. It's extremely popular on the planets of the Trading League, despite having been banned on all but two planets because of its extremely intoxicating characteristic with respect to most of the inhabitants. In his distribution business, Farpel conveniently ignored this little detail. As for the permitted planets, the beings inhabiting Walinga 7 and Hoolit 2 didn't have any notable physical reaction to Biepal, so it really wasn't worth selling there anyway. Curiously, the inhabitants of Walinga 7 and Hoolit 2 are already renowned for their extraordinary lack of inhibitions, with the rather curious habit of prancing through the galaxy *sans* clothing, but that's another topic for a different day. As a further aside, it's worth noting that there was actually a small sales volume of Biepal on Hoolit 2, but only for use as rocket fuel to enhance their fireworks displays on major holidays.

The other planetary populations of the Trading League often enjoyed a discreet vessel of Biepal now and again, even though it was illegal on their planets. For example, Korpits often indulged before a party or other exciting event on their world (it tended to make Korpits behave in a rather silly fashion, so they didn't really care if the event turned out to be a dud). Female Chienolians, on the other hand, were often seen to be sneaking a glass or two during their renowned gong concerts, which, for reasons unknown, the male Chienolians found to be utterly thrilling, while the female Chienolians thought them to be an utter bore. Apparently, the Biepal allowed the female Chienolians to sleep while keeping their eyes wide open, thus allowing them to look extremely interested in the concert while squeezing in a nice nap at the same time.

Brobding was intrigued; he thought that Earth might actually represent a real possibility for Biepal sales. In his brief exposure to the population, he observed that several of the local inhabitants had seemed extremely hostile and tense. He thought that Biepal might be just the ticket to get the indigenous population to relax. "I think that could be a really interesting opportunity, Farpel! But do you think it might violate any of their laws?"

Farpel gave Brobding a look of disdain, or as close to that as a Kinglorf can manage. "Meas, are you going to start up again with the legal annoyances? Legal, schmeegal! If there's an interest, we should pursue it; we can deal with the rule monkeys later."

Brobding had a feeling that this would be Farpel's attitude; he resigned himself to working within Farpel's ethical framework, or lack thereof, if he wanted to make any progress. "All right, Farpel, how do you suggest we proceed?"

Farpel was busy slurping up more beverage through his straws, so it took a moment before he answered. "I would say that the first step is to get in touch with that Mrs. Hensworthy friend of yours, and get her take on the deal. If we're going to go Barnork-wide with this stuff, she's going to be the easiest starting point. See what she says, and if it sounds promising, let's set up a meet."

"I'm sending you a Holo-CalloMatic link; you can reach out to me on that, but keep it to yourself, Meas."

With an initial plan in place, Brobding and Farpel disconnected. Brobding heard Kolameas Elwinkem in the background as they signed off; she appeared to be continuing her considerable observations on the subject of sand.

2

Eleanora Hensworthy and her husband Malthorp were having a fairly quiet day at home. It had been raining for seemingly days in Hampsthwaite, where she and Malthorp resided in a comfortable little cottage. Luckily, the fireplace in the living room took off some of the chill.

As you may recall, Malthorp was a Jordalakian, who happened to arrive on the local planet some 25 Earth years earlier, on a sociological expedition. His vessel then had some navigation issues, and he couldn't manage to find his way back to the interdimensional portal that would have allowed him to return home. He had parked himself in Mrs. Hensworthy's back garden to check the glove compartment for a map, but all he found were a few travel brochures and some crumbs from the previous occupant's snacks. Mrs. Hensworthy then happened upon him as he was rummaging. Having little choice, he decided to stay.

Jordalakians have a particular skill that can be quite useful on occasion: they are shape-shifters, whose native form might be described as a gelatinous mass. There was a downside to this aspect of Malthorp's physicality, however; he tended to swell up a bit when the weather was particularly humid. He was residing in a chair near the fire, with an appearance rather resembling a parade balloon, reading travel brochures related to some particularly dry vacation locales, and hoping the fire in the fireplace would knock down the humidity enough for him to return to his normal Malthorpian form. Mrs. Hensworthy sat in the chair opposite him, reading a book on the *Care and Feeding of the Domesticated Philodendron Plant*.

As they sat before the fire, dwelling on their respective interests, a familiar whooshing sound made itself known, and became louder and louder. At the same time, a whirling grayish vortex appeared as a small spot, and began growing in the doorway of the Hensworthy's walk-through bookcase, a doorway that ordinarily opened to the kitchen. The Hensworthys calmly observed the proceedings with interest, as they had become accustomed to this particular interruption of their day.

Moments later, Brobding Measelfort, Mrs. Hensworthy's favorite Measeloot, stepped through an interdimensional rift that now formed a doorway of its own between the transdimensional transport tube in which Brobding had been standing, and the Hensworthy's living room.

Just a brief reminder: Some months earlier, at least from the Earthling's perspective, Brobding had been repairing damage to the wall of this particular transdimensional transport tube when the wall gave way, and formed a rift into Mrs. Hensworthy's living room through the middle of her walk-through bookcase. Various introductions had ensued. But let's get back to the present.

Mrs. Hensworthy was delighted. "Why, Mr. Measelfort! How nice to see you again!" Strange and squeaky sounds emanated from Brobding Measelfort as he made several odd gestures with multiple appendages.

"Oh, yes, the translator! I can never seem to remember." Mrs. Hensworthy reached around to a side table which was, oddly enough, at her side, opened a drawer, drew forth a GadgiYack, and placed it in one of her nostrils. As you know, the GadgiYack, placed in any convenient nostril, allows one being to instantly understand the language and manner of expression of another being. As for manners themselves, however, the GadgiYack doesn't have much to offer in that arena.

"I'm certainly glad we have these gadgets handy!" she noted as she handed another GadgiYack to Malthorp. Given his somewhat swollen condition, he had a bit of trouble placing it in his own nostril.

Brobding was now completely intelligible. "Greetings, Hensworthys! I trust I'm not interrupting anything of vital importance? Oh, and not to be too annoying on the subject, but it's 'GadgiYack,' not 'gadget,' Mrs. Hensworthy."

Malthorp was having some difficulty speaking at the moment, due to his notably inflated condition, so Mrs. Hensworthy spoke right up. "Oh, yes, dear, I'm aware. 'Gadget' is sort of a catch-all phrase we use to refer to various mechanical and electronic doohickeys and what-nots."

The terms 'doohickey' and 'what-not' did not serve to clarify the conversation for Brobding, but he diplomatically accepted the explanation, and proceeded onward.

"I was hoping we might speak about a new product venture that's presented itself, courtesy of our mutual acquaintance Farpel."

The Hensworthys were listening with interest. "Oh, yes? What is that nice Mr. Farpel up to these days?"

"Well, he's been distributing a beverage called Biepal to a number of planets in the Trading League, and we were wondering if your fellow beings here on Barnork 3, or rather, Earth, might have an interest in trying it."

By this time, the fireplace was beginning to have a positive effect on Malthorp's humidity issue. He had deflated to the point where he managed to sit up in the chair, and get his oral orifice working. "Hello, Brobding; sorry, I was a bit indisposed there for a while. You're probably aware that Jordalakians and humidity don't mix very well. A question comes to mind: what sort of beverage is this Biepal, and how is it derived? We need to consider how the indigenous fauna might react to the stuff."

Brobding reached through the rift behind him, and withdrew a small bottle from a satchel he had there. "I brought along a small sample provided by Farpel, and thought you might like to try it. I should mention that it's rather intoxicating to most of the beings in the Trading League, and the Chienolians have a tendency to fall asleep when they indulge in it."

Mrs. Hensworthy interjected quickly, "Now, Malthorp, do be careful. You know how you react when you've had too much sherry before dinner. Brobding, dear, Malthorp unfortunately tends to revert to his gelatinous Jordalakian form when the alcoholic beverages flow a bit too freely. The last time he over-indulged, he rolled down the front of the chair, and resided in a puddle, or perhaps I should say *as* a puddle, on the carpet for quite several hours. It was somewhat disconcerting."

"Have no fear, my dear, I'll take only the most cursory sip of the beverage." With that, Malthorp took the bottle from Brobding, opened the top, and poured a small amount into his now-empty teacup. He examined it carefully, and attempted to ascertain if the beverage had any discernible odor. "It seems to have somewhat of a fruity bouquet."

"Yes, it's derived from the juice of the biepalfruit, which is only known to grow on the Whoola Planets."

Malthorp looked uncomfortable at the mention of the Whoola Planets. "I'm acquainted with that planetary system; Whoola 4a and 4b are on opposite sides of the star in that system, and are both basically rainforest planets. Some Jordalakians have been known to go there as a rest cure, since they can only remain in a rather inflated gelatinous form with all that humidity, but it always made me feel annoyingly out of control somehow."

Malthorp tasted the beverage, and contemplated the flavor briefly. "Very nice, very fruity. I believe it would be considered a bit on the strong side, compared to the usual beverages found

here. Would you care to try some, my dear?"
He passed the teacup to Mrs. Hensworthy.

"Well, I'm not in the habit of imbibing
intoxicating beverages, mind you, but in the
interests of research..." And with that, Mrs.
Hensworthy downed a fair swallow of the
beverage, and started coughing.

She managed to comment between coughs, in a
fairly raspy voice. "Oh, yes,"...cough, choke,
cough... "Very fruity, indeed! Not......particularly
my......cup of tea, mind you!" She reached for
her own teacup, and proceeded to down the
contents. "There, that's better. It's a bit strong
for me, I should say, but I would imagine it
might be very popular indeed in some of the
seedier drinking establishments!"

Malthorp admonished her, "Now, now, let us not
judge. I'm sure there are any number of beings
on this planet who would find Biepal to be quite
enjoyable." He addressed Brobding. "You did
say that you might have an interest in offering
Biepal here, is that right?"

Brobding nodded in ascent.

"Well, Brobding, let us discuss this among ourselves, and consider how we might be of assistance. Does that work for you, my dear?" As he spoke, Malthorp's ears started to droop toward the arms of the chair.

Mrs. Hensworthy took note. "Malthorp, honestly, I asked you to be careful; now look what that beverage has done!"

Malthorp observed his earlobes now resting upon the cushions of the armrests. "Yes, well, I suppose that Biepal was a bit stronger than I had anticipated. Not to worry; I'm sure I'll be completely returned to Malthorpian form in short order. In any case, Brobding, give us a few earthly rotations to discuss the matter, and drop back in for a chat. Oh, and do feel free to invite Mr. Farpel to join us. If there are plans to be made, it would tend to simplify things if we're all in the same room."

3

Approximately 4.62 earthly rotations later, Brobding Measelfort happened to be working in a transdimensional transport tube in the vicinity of the Grange planets. A group of Towlak school kids had passed through this particular tube on a field trip, and, as is their wont, left claw marks all over the walls. For those unacquainted with the Towlaks, they rather resemble a lobster with six appendages, and apparently the species has forgotten the function of the common nail clipper.

It was one of Brobding's jobs to remove or camouflage the unsightly marks. Luckily, on the one hand, the walls of a transdimensional transport tube can be readily repaired with transdimensional concrete. Unfortunately, on the other hand, the cost of transdimensional concrete had gone through the roof lately, so word had come down from the main office that repair crews were to use it as efficiently as possible. In an earlier age, Brobding would have slathered a bunch of the stuff on the tube wall, smoothed it out, and WOINK! The tube would have looked as good as new. Now, he had to carefully trowel the concrete into each crevice left by unruly Towlak claws. It took a while.

Brobding was just about done for the day, and was seriously considering going to dinner on Grange 5; he had heard there was a particularly good Measeloot restaurant there that served a really fine smoked gridnap salad, with the horns ever so carefully removed.

As it turned out, the Grange planets were accessed by two different transdimensional transport tubes; the second such access happened to be the transport tube that was dimensionally adjacent to the Barnork system, and therefore, Mrs. Hensworthy's living room. That is, assuming one could create an interdimensional portal in the wall of the tube. And since Brobding was an expert in tube repair, he happened to be just such a one.

Since he was in the vicinity, and several earth days had already passed by, he thought he'd try dropping in on the Hensworthys to see if they had given proper consideration to his Biepal distribution proposal.

Suddenly, he remembered that the Hensworthys asked to include Farpel in the next meeting. He reached for his Holo-CalloMatic, and activated the link Farpel had provided to him.

A few buzzy sounds later, Farpel's 3-dimensional projection appeared in front of Brobding. "Hey, Meas. On our way to a party; what's up?"

"Greetings, Farpel; I trust you're doing well! The Hensworthys were hoping we might gather for a discussion on the Biepal opportunity. I'm going there now to see if they're up for a chat. Any chance you can join us?"

One of Kolameas Elwinkem's rather large appendages was visible on the edge of Farpel's image as she waved it around, and Brobding could hear her chattering about something to do with party dresses, but the specifics weren't clear. "I'll tell you what, Meas; you check out the Hensworthy situation first. If they're ready to get serious, call me back, and I'll find a way to get there. By that time, I'll probably be bored with the party anyway. Later!" And with that, Farpel disconnected.

'He is a rather abrupt sort, isn't he?' thought Brobding as he proceeded to the transdimensional transport tube that would provide access to that particularly useful region in the middle of the Hensworthy bookcase.

Arriving at the appropriate locale, Brobding withdrew a portable particle collider from his tool box, and cranked it up. In short order, he had formed a micro-singularity, which he then used to vacuum up the matter in its immediate vicinity, namely, the material that formed the nearby wall of the tube. This created a miniscule rift in the tube wall, which proceeded to grow until it was large enough for Brobding to pass through it. At that point, he transferred the micro-singularity to a spherical vessel, with a magnetic field that would effectively contain it, and returned all his goodies and the now-tamed singularity to his tool box.

There, on the other side of the rift, he saw Mrs. Hensworthy's husband Malthorp enjoying a cup of tea in the living room. Malthorp watched attentively as Brobding stepped through the rift;

Mrs. Hensworthy did not appear to be present, but Brobding heard her voice from elsewhere in the space.

"Shall I refresh your tea, dear? I imagine it may be getting a bit of a chill by now."

Having a certain awareness of multi-dimensional phenomena, Malthorp thought it best to let Mrs. Hensworthy know that they had a visitor. "Ah, do be careful with the bookcase doorway, my dear. Our friend Mr. Measelfort has made an appearance, and I recall that you may not be able to see his interdimensional portal from your side of the bookcase opening. We don't want you tripping over the 2-dimensional edge of the opening now, do we?"

Mrs. Hensworthy came around the corner from the kitchen into the living room. "Oh, hello, Mr. Measelfort! Thank you for letting me know, Malthorp. You're quite right; one can't actually see the rift from the other side. I'm still getting accustomed to that oddity. But if I can't see it, what is it exactly that I would trip over?"

Malthorp pondered the implications briefly. "Quite interesting, that. The side of the portal facing Mr. Measelfort's dimensional domain exists in a different 3-space from our own, and therefore can't be discerned by us at all, whereas the side of the portal facing our dimensional domain is quite obvious. Most curious, indeed! As to what you would trip over, it would be the two-dimensional edge of the rift opening as it appears from the living room side of the doorway; as you progressed through the doorway and past the rift opening, you'd fall over the edge that exists as a 2-dimensional plane in our 3-space; or perhaps it should be considered 1-dimensional, as it has only length in our space; all its other aspects reside in Mr. Measelfort's 3-space. In any case, we're being rude to our guest. How are you, my friend?"

A series of squeaks and whistles in a broad frequency range issued forth from Brobding as he gesticulated rather generously.

"Oh, for goodness sakes! Malthorp, do take out the GadgiYacks! I just can't seem to remember to put the thing in my nose!"

Malthorp withdrew two GadgiYacks from the drawer of the adjacent table, and he and Mrs.

Hensworthy positioned them as required. Brobding smiled.

"Thank you, Hensworthys; it does get somewhat frustrating when one tries to communicate without modern technology. I'm glad I found you at home, and was wondering if you've had time to consider the conversation we had earlier regarding Biepal?"

Just as Brobding raised the subject, a distinctive whirling mass appeared at the ceiling of the Hensworthy's living room, a rift appeared in the center of the mass, and Dearlotin Farpelmop floated down to the floor, using the lighter-than-air flotation sacs conveniently located on each side of his torso.

"What's up, Hensworthys? Hey, Meas. I left a microsensor on this side of the rift the last time I visited. It detects certain energy signatures, to let me know in case an interdimensional disturbance occurred here in my absence, so I kind of figured you had shown up. The party on Wowserlik 3 got boring to the point where even a Chienolian gong concert would have seemed exciting in comparison, so I decided to drop in, so to speak. Besides, they were serving gridnap, and I'm allergic to anything with horns. So where do we stand on the Biepal situation?"

Mrs. Hensworthy chimed in, "Well, hello to you, Mr. Farpel! We were just about to broach that subject. Malthorp and I made some delicate inquiries, and we believe we've found an interested party who is willing to distribute your Biepal. Malthorp, dear, why don't you elaborate for us?"

"I would be delighted, my dear. With our particular interest in sherry, I've made acquaintance with the proprietor of a lovely bottle shop in Harrogate. After a discreet discussion, she proceeded to introduce me to a boutique distributor of alcoholic beverages operating out of London, with various connections overseas and on the continent. They, in turn, would like to try a case of Biepal, and introduce some of their key customers to the product. If it seems to be of interest, they would be pleased to discuss a distribution arrangement."

Farpel looked at them as if they had suddenly burst into flame. "Are you serious?! What kind of planet is this, anyway?! Listen, I kinda don't work that way. On the planets in the Trading League, my boys make a few connections, and their connections make a few connections, and then we open a whole lot of interdimensional rifts in just the right places, and we drop the stuff off. Then we go back and get paid the same way. That way, we cut out the middle guy; you know what I mean?"

Malthorp was a bit taken aback. "Yes, Mr. Farpel, I understand fully. Don't you think it might be just a bit awkward, though, if a being such as yourself suddenly made an appearance in many different locales on this planet? Come, come now. Brobding, you have some inkling as to the nature of the locale fauna. How do you think they would react if Mr. Farpel were to suddenly drop from the ceiling into their shops?"

Brobding shuddered noticeably. "I think the indigenous beings would believe that they're facing an alien invasion!"

Malthorp smiled. "Exactly. As much as we admire your business acumen, Mr. Farpel, I'm afraid we really can't have Kinglorfs showing up around the planet uninvited. There would be chaos!"

Farpel tried to not take the comment personally; he thought about it for a moment. "Ok, I get it, I get it; from the perspective of these local backward yahoos, I'm a giant talking dog with four extra arms and a lotta teeth. So I'll tell you what; I'll give you guys a case for the distributor guy. When he's totally wowed, which I know he'll be, then you get me some particular locations from this guy, and tell him that you'll get the Biepal delivered to those places; I'll tell you when that will happen. You tell him we can drop it anywhere, anytime, no problem. He should be thrilled; no shipping costs! He doesn't really need to know about the interdimensional part of the program, now, does he? Once we're in business, we'll drop the stuff, the guy will pay you for the goods, and you'll get my share of the value to me."

"I kind of remember that the last time, we had that little problem with, uh, 'medium of exchange.' I still don't know what you guys use for trade here, and you guys apparently don't know very much about guaackles, korpitwinkies, storts, or spunod, which just about *everybody* else uses these days to, shall we say, lubricate the wheels of commerce, so we'll have to use something else. I know you guys like diamonds, but they're just trinkets in the rest of the galaxy."

"I did a little, shall we say, 'research,' and you guys have something growing here that is really, really rare among the Trading League planets. If you can get me those, they'll be worth real value to me on the other planets. I think you call them 'carrots.' So for each delivery, I'll get you the juice, and you get me a good-sized collection of carrots."

Malthorp and Mrs. Hensworthy looked at each other for a long moment; Malthorp was the first to react. "Let me see if I have this right; you want us to pay you your share in carrots, is that right?"

"That's right, carrots." Mrs. Hensworthy excused herself from the room briefly, and disappeared toward the kitchen as Farpel continued. "And the good stuff, not the pitiful little ones. And Meas, I'll make sure you get a cut of the action for opening up the territory, so to speak."

Mrs. Hensworthy reappeared a moment later; in her hand, she held a large bunch of healthy carrots that she had acquired earlier that day at the local grocer's. Each carrot displayed a substantial length and girth. "Is this what you had in mind, Mr. Farpel?"

Farpel's eyes went wide as he looked at the vegetables displayed before him; he made a concerted effort not to drool. It took him a moment before he could react. "Yeah, lady, I would say that, given the demand in the Trading League, your average Kinglorf could comfortably retire on a few bunches like that. Of course, I ain't your average Kinglorf." He proceeded to smirk. "You get me goods like that, and we're good. So, are we good?"

The Hensworthys looked at each other, and at Brobding. Everyone smiled, and Malthorp offered a response. "I think we're good."

4

Several weeks later (from an Earthly perspective), Farpel had provided a case of Biepal to the Hensworthys. They, in turn, provided it to the distributor, who, as anticipated, absolutely loved it, comparing it to a fine wine. They placed a big order.

The operation then started in earnest, first in the United Kingdom, and then on to the European continent. The distributor provided a list of bottle shops to which Farpel was to deliver the goods, and overnight, one might even say magically, the bottles appeared *inside* the doorway of each shop. The shop owners were a bit perturbed at first, to say the least, as to how the delivery people managed to get the cases into their shops *even though the shops were closed*, but the distributor gave them substantial reassurances, and they accepted the state of affairs for the time being, happy to be getting a new and exciting product to offer. Of course, the fact that Biepal represented a stupendous profit opportunity for the distributor and shops had absolutely nothing to do with their positive response; but it didn't hurt.

Of a sudden, and much to the surprise of the distributor as well as the Hensworthys, a mysterious advertisement began showing up online, as well as in the real world:

Are you people *Biepal People?*

Unbeknownst to them, Farpel had created the ad, and then engaged with some shady Kinglorf associates of his, who proceeded to hack the Earth internet, as well as the electronic billboards lining various highways, in order to give the ads some exposure. Unfortunately, Farpel had based the advertising image on the inhabitants of Zorbel 4, who happen to have the most extraordinarily long arms in this galactic neighborhood. Luckily, no one seemed to notice.

People started making inquiries to find out exactly what this *Biepal* was. Internet queries regarding Biepal absolutely soared into the *millions*. Subsequently, Biepal sales were brisk.

Meanwhile, the Earth continued its usual rotation about its axis, as well as completing about 21.382 degrees of arc in revolving about the sun.

At the Royal London Hospital, Dr. Worthing Helfington, General Practitioner, was working his usual evening shift, responding to the usual range of mishaps, injuries, and other concerns, as well as the typical collection of hypochondriacs and crazies who showed up each day claiming to be growing extra arms, or experiencing a new and exciting disease, when a most unusual case presented itself. At first, Dr. Helfington wasn't sure if this case fell into the area of 'other concerns,' or if perhaps it was more appropriate to the 'crazies' categorization.

Ralph and Nora Vanligfolken were a normal middle-aged couple living in a normal suburban enclave. Ralph was a somewhat portly accountant, ordinarily about 5 feet 8 inches tall on a good day, with hair that had thinned over the years, and wore horn-rimmed glasses of some notable thickness due to his exceptional nearsightedness, from reading too many accounting forms. Ralph was also often seen to be wearing hats. He was of reasonably good health, except for a bunion on his left foot that annoyed him occasionally.

Nora had also put on a few extra pounds here and there over the years, but did her best to maintain her appearance, always dressing smartly. She was in the same general vicinity as her husband height-wise, and had an especially pointy nose, which we mention for no particular reason other than its notable prominence. Her health was also in the reasonable realm, although Nora did enjoy complaining about this or that ache just about every day.

They had been hesitant to go to the hospital this particular day; after all, they weren't actually feeling ill in any way. They were, however, experiencing some very odd bodily changes. What was even odder was that they should both be experiencing the same change, for no reason they could discern. You see, they were getting taller.

"I tell you, doctor, it's the strangest thing. At first, I was convinced it was the imagination. But then, the other morning, I put on me pants, and they don't reach to me ankles! Then the missus and me, we get in the automobile for a drive to the shops, and I have to adjust the mirrors! I haven't adjusted the mirrors going on, what would you say, Nora, twenty year? And I actually had to move the seat back! I didn't even know how; had to look it up in the manual!"

"Yes, dear, I think it was when you tried those elevator shoes back twenty two year now. You moved the seat so the pedals would work just so, and then moved the mirrors because you moved the seat, and I seem to recall that the steering wheel was then too far away. Thank goodness you gave those shoes away to that short cousin Bellamy of yours."

"And doctor, I've been finding changes of my own. Why, I was in the kitchen just yesterday, and needed to take down our pet cat from the top shelf of the cupboard, where he managed to make himself comfortable. I usually get out the small step stool in order to get a hold of Schlemiel, that's his name, Schlemiel, named after a favorite uncle of mine, but, well, today, I just reached up and grabbed him! I believe he was as surprised as I was. The ceiling is definitely getting closer, I tell you!"

Dr. Helfington was perplexed. His first task was to measure the Vanligfokens to get a baseline on their height. They were now both in the vicinity of six feet tall.

He proceeded to ask the questions one might expect under such circumstances: Did the Vanligfolkens eat anything unusual lately? Any exposure to chemicals or other substances? Any insect or other bites or scratches? Any travel to foreign countries? Any gamma-ray blasts from sinister-looking characters?

Ralph and Nora couldn't remember anything unusual in those departments. There was their neighbor, Helen Loonwickey, who kept claiming that aliens were reading her mind through her chimney, but they couldn't see the relevance of that to their current condition.

Ralph had a thought. "I understand there's some strange effects if you get bit by a radioactive spider! Do you think that might have something to do with it, doctor?"

As Dr. Helfington was not particularly an aficionado of comic books, he missed the reference. "Do you think you may have been bitten by a spider in that condition, Mr. Vanligfolken?"

Ralph had to admit that he didn't think it likely. "Haven't seen any radioactive spiders about, as far as I know, but you just never know."

The doctor had no choice but to follow standard practice. "Well, Mr. and Mrs. Vanligfolken, I think we should run a series of tests, and see if anything interesting shows up. In the meantime, please try to remember if there have been any changes in your day-to-day activities and indulgences recently."

As the doctor typed in some notes, and arranged for blood samples and other tests, Nora was ruminating on their recent activities. "You know, Ralph, there is that Biepal."

The doctor's ears perked up, although this would have been considerably more noticeable on, for instance, a Chienolian, whose ears are approximately 16 inches long by Earth measurements. "Excuse me, Mrs. Vanligfolken, but what is Biepal?"

Nora responded with enthusiasm. "Oh, well, doctor, Biepal! It's this lovely new beverage we discovered recently at our local bottle shop. It has just the nicest fruity flavor. We've been having some every evening now. It's practically addictive!"

Dr. Helfington was really interested now. "Practically addictive, you say? Perhaps you could provide me with a sample; I'd be interested to see what sort of properties it has."

Ralph considered the request. "I think we have an open bottle we might bring round; wouldn't you say, Nora?"

"Yes, dear, I put it in the fridge because you said you like it cold, and also because Schlemiel... Did I mention that's our cat, doctor? Schlemiel kept trying to lick the bottle! We'll bring it round tomorrow for you. But be careful; you're going to enjoy it!"

5

The next day, Nora Vanligfolken was back to the doctor's office with a bottle of Biepal. It was almost empty, but there was still enough for a nice afternoon aperitif, or perhaps for a little laboratory experimentation. Nora appeared somewhat agitated as she was once again ushered into the doctor's examination room.

"Oh, doctor! The most astonishing thing has happened! I think this must be it!"

Dr. Helfington offered his most concerned look. "Indeed! Good morning Mrs. Vanligfolken, please sit down. What is it that's happened, and what must be it?"

Nora passed the bottle to the doctor. "Well, doctor, remember when I mentioned yesterday that Schlemiel, that's our cat, you know, Schlemiel, well, he kept licking the bottle, and so I placed it in the fridge? Well, now Schlemiel appears to have grown to twice his original size! I'm telling you, doctor, he's the size of a cocker spaniel at this point, and I must say, that's not doing his litter box any favors!"

The doctor's eyes went wide as he stared at the bottle of Biepal. Of course, he was only human, so his eyes didn't go as wide as, say, the Wortelukes of Pleebus 6 (which is not to be confused with Pleebus 3, to which one often refers simply as 'Pleebus'). Wortelukes enjoy living in rather poorly lit cave-homes underground, as a lightbulb monopoly on Pleebus 6 has resulted in fairly outrageous prices for the things. Their eyes, in human terms, are rather almond shaped, approximately the size of your average party balloon, and are renowned to be the largest, and therefore widest, in this particular portion of the galaxy. Accordingly, on the occasion of a Worteluke requiring corrective glasses, the invoices from the opticians on Pleebus 6 also tend to be the largest in that same region. But let's get back to our story.

"I'm going to run a series of tests on this Biepal and see what we can find out, Mrs. Vanligfolken. In the meantime, I suggest you and your husband refrain from indulging in any more of this substance."

Nora wore a rather forlorn expression. "Oh, dear, Ralph and I have grown quite fond of the beverage; I'll do my best to convince him, doctor, but I can't make any promises. Do let me know if you discover anything interesting in your inquiries."

Dr. Helfington proceeded to examine in detail both the Biepal, and the various samples of body fluids he had acquired from the Vanligfolkens. He was stumped.

"There must be chemicals in here I can't identify with the technologies we have available. I simply can't understand how it is that the Vanligfolkens are getting taller from this. And their cat is getting larger! It's a conundrum."

He was sitting behind his desk, discussing the matter with his associate, Dr. Bilford Wrankle, who resided on the sofa in Dr. Helfington's office. Wrankle wrinkled his brow in thought. "Well, Worthing, perhaps it's time to call in the big troops. There's that government lab that we've worked with since, oh, it must be the 1940's, when our predecessors were worried about chemicals used during the war. Maybe they can figure something out."

It was Helfington's turn to wrinkle his brow. "I thought about that, Bilford, but you know what's going to happen if they find anything of interest. Suddenly, it becomes a military project, and we're left on the sidelines."

Wrankle commiserated. "I know, but I don't see that we have much choice on this. If this stuff, what did you call it? Biepal? If this Biepal turns out to have unusual properties, I think we need to know about it before we have some sort of epidemic on our hands."

"An epidemic of tallness?" Helfington smiled. "We should bottle the stuff ourselves and sell it to people who think they're too short, which is probably about half the population. But I get your point; I suppose I'll call the lab and see what they can do." Wrankle tried his best not to take the 'people who think they're too short' comment personally, as he stood about five foot two inches tall in his platform shoes.

After a quick phone call to a Dr. Curiotis, Dr. Helfington whisked off a sample of Biepal to FriendlyLabs, which resided in an unassuming suburb just outside of London. For security purposes, the suburb shall remain nameless, though we can tell you that the name of the suburb starts with the letter C, and has a fairly good pastry shop in its town center; as a matter of fact, we can highly recommend the orange almond brioche. But we've told you too much already.

FriendlyLabs was located in an ordinary little storefront, and at first glance, offered various laboratory services to a range of local veterinary clinics. In the back, however, was an entirely different story.

You see, FriendlyLabs was a façade for a highly sophisticated and top secret government facility, with laboratory and diagnostic capabilities that were beyond the imaginations of the most complete publicly available laboratories in the world.

The Biepal sample arrived promptly, prominently marked as "Stool sample for Fluffers, 3 year old golden retriever," in keeping with the laboratory's cover story. Dr. Curiotis assigned its evaluation to one of her most talented laboratory technicians, Nicole Pipette, who was on loan from a similar secret facility in France. Within 10 days (at least based on

Earthly rotations), Ms. Pipette handed a file marked "Top Secret" to Dr. Curiotis, and they discussed the data briefly.

"I am finding these chemistries most vexing and intriguing, Madam Doctor, most vexing and intriguing. Indeed, I have never seen this particular formulation before. I shall continue in my pursuit; perhaps something I can recognize will reveal itself."

Dr. Curiotis wasn't too happy with this. "Well, Pipette, you're the best we have. If you can't draw something useful out of this, no one can. And we really need to get some answers; I've been told in confidence that this substance is having some strange effects on the population, and we need to understand it as soon as possible."

"Merci, Madam Doctor! I shall endeavor to do my best. If I may ask, what are these 'strange effects' of which you speak?"

Curiotis paused for a moment before answering. She then spoke in a low tone. "Pipette, you need to keep this to yourself, but...apparently, and you may find this all quite unbelievable... it's making people *taller*."

Pipette looked at Dr. Curiotis as if she had lost her mind. "Taller, you say? Taller, as in... taller? With the greater, how do you say, height? Further from the *sol*, excusé moi, ground? *Incroyable!*"

"That's right, and I need you to keep this quiet. If it gets out, we could have a panic on our hands."

"*Certainement*, Madam Doctor! I tell no one!" However, in the back of her mind, Nicole Pipette was having some interesting thoughts of her own. It's worth noting that Ms. Pipette was quite a petite figure, managing to reach a maximum height of 4 feet 10 inches, and that was with the rather stylish heels she wore. Interesting thoughts, indeed.

Meanwhile, back in Hampsthwaite, Farpel and the Hensworthys continued to work on distribution channels for Biepal, unaware of the government's newfound interest in their beverage.

Mrs. Hensworthy was particularly excited as she sat in her living with her husband Malthorp. Farpel had just joined them by dropping into their home through his usual means, an interdimensional rift in the living room ceiling.

"Well, now, gentlemen, I'm pleased to announce that our distributor out of London has made some very useful contacts in the United States of America, and we should be able to deliver our product to various bottle stores there almost immediately. I believe they refer to them as 'liquor stores,' but it's the same concept. Mr. Farpel, do you think you can keep up on the supply side?"

Farpel wore a look of confidence as he replied to Mrs. Hensworthy, although it's hard to discern that look on a Kinglorf, since they tend to be a very confident species as a rule. "Don't worry about that, lady. You just get me the coordinates, and I'll make sure the stuff gets dropped off."

6

"Did you see this article? This article in The Guardian?" Malthorp was sitting in the living room on a Saturday evening, addressing Mrs. Hensworthy, who was just coming from the kitchen.

"Which article is that, dear?" Mrs. Hensworthy had brought some tea with her, and sat down in her favorite chair. "I haven't seen The Guardian today."

Malthorp passed her the tablet upon which he was reading the news. "This one, the one about people getting taller. It just struck me as quite odd."

Mrs. Hensworthy quickly scanned the text. "Well, if it's in The Guardian, it's probably true. There's so much garbage news these days, I don't know what to believe. What is it that attracted you to this particular piece of news?"

Malthorp considered the content for a few minutes. "I don't know, exactly; perhaps it's the timing of the event, or the geographic distribution. From the description provided, it seems to me that this 'taller' business aligns rather nicely with our introduction of Biepal to these various areas." His brow was notably wrinkled at this point; it seemed to happen quite often when people discussed Biepal. Perhaps it was another side effect.

"Oh, I'm sure that's a coincidence, dear. I can't imagine Biepal is making anyone taller! It's just an interesting beverage!"

Mrs. Hensworthy's response did nothing to change the wrinkle in Malthorp's brow. "Yes, Eleanora, but it's an interesting beverage with extraterrestrial origins. You remember what tea can do to certain other species, and you even saw an example with your own eyes. And that was just tea!"

It was Mrs. Hensworthy's turn to be concerned. "Oh, dear, you don't really think it's the Biepal, do you? I mean, making people taller, of all things!"

At about the same time (that is, taking into account the time zone difference), in an obscure office at the Pentagon in the United States of America, General Borkland Dithering sat in his office on that same Saturday, sporting a wrinkle in *his* brow that was remarkably similar to Malthorp's. On this particular morning, it was raining in Arlington, Virginia, where the five-sided Pentagon edifice resided, and his outlook was as dark as the clouds outside of the building.

He had just finished reading a top secret report on a new substance that had made its way into the public domain, and he found its purported effects on the population rather worrisome. Of even greater concern was that no one could seem to pinpoint the origin of the substance.

Borkland Archibald Dithering had worked his way up the ranks in the armed forces, beginning his military career as a sergeant in an officers' mess hall. By contending in detail with what the military considered as 'food,' Dithering had learned a great deal about chemistry.

He was now in charge of a secretive program known as the Toxicology Evaluation and eXistential Threat INvestigations Group, well known, by those who swam in these particular classified waters, by its acronym, TEXTING. It was buried so deep inside the Pentagon that even the top brass only knew about it on a need-to-know basis. And those involved in the program felt that most top brass didn't need to know. The floor on which it resided didn't even have an elevator button; you had to press the '6' and 'Door Open' buttons at the same time for the elevator to get there, and even that only worked if you said the term "wiener schnitzel" out loud in a sing-songy voice at the same time as you pressed the buttons. The program didn't show up on government budgets; it was funded through a few select inventions that were licensed for public use, like the formulation for the odd substance used to make gummy bears, and the software for certain recognizably addictive video games that can't be named here, but whose names may possibly start with the letter G or M.

Just as Dithering finished the report, a phone on his desk rang. It was the secure line, and it startled him for a moment, as he didn't often receive calls on the secure line on a Saturday. He just looked at the phone briefly, as if it was suddenly radioactive, and then picked up the receiver. It was one of his key aides, Colonel Crassik. "General Dithering, I'm glad I reached you. I was just reviewing the report on this Biepal substance, and was hoping you've had a chance to peruse the same report. I'd appreciate your thoughts, sir."

"Ah, Colonel Crassik. Yes, I just completed the report myself. Quite astonishing, I would say. It seems measurable portions of the population are getting taller at an alarming rate. I understand from my sources at the Cottage that they've been getting calls and emails from every imaginable corner of the economy about this phenomenon. Apparently, it's become quite disruptive."

A little background might be helpful here. First, the 'Cottage' to which General Dithering referred would be The White House, the very core of the Executive Branch of Government in the United States. Every titan of industry who ever made a campaign contribution to the current occupant of The White House was calling to find out what was going on with this 'height business.'

Second, it's worth noting that Farpel, Brobding and the Hensworthys had introduced Biepal just about all over the world approximately six months before General Dithering had a chance to review the top secret report on its effects, a report dutifully prepared by his staff. There really was no report to see prior to this, as increases in height only began showing up about three months after people started enjoying Biepal. At this point, as far as General Dithering and his staff knew, they were the only ones who had definitively made the connection between Biepal and this height phenomenon.

"Yes, Crassik, we may have the beginnings of a real crisis on our hands. From what I see in this report, subjects who are regularly inoculated with this substance, in one way or another, start to grow within three months of exposure, and, so far, just keep growing. There are reports of people who are now nine feet tall, and we have no idea how far this will go. This could be some sort of subversive plot, and we need to get on top of it fast."

The gentlemen took some time to consider in silence what the general had just said. Then

Dithering had some additional thoughts on the subject. "On the other hand, Crassik, I can definitely see some value to this, if we can get it under our own control. Aside from being able to see over everyone else at parades, it could be useful to have a subset of our folks in the armed forces who are particularly tall. And basketball teams are going to go mad for this stuff!" He chuckled, and Crassik obediently chuckled in unison with him. "As for the rest of the economy, well, if this keeps up, I see some serious upheaval on the horizon; at the very least, builders are going to need new standards for ceiling height."

"Well, General, what are your orders for our next actions?"

General Dithering stared at the wall briefly. "Crassik, I think it's time for you to get me an appointment with the President."

While the General was working through channels to meet with the President of the United States on the subject of Biepal, the media was keeping busy indeed. As I'm sure you know, there's nothing quite like a good disaster to get the media excited. And if a situation isn't quite a disaster yet, the media will always work hard on behalf of the public to ensure that whatever is happening is properly perceived as a disaster in the works.

This situation was no different, and from certain perspectives, there really were some substantial consequences as a result of the population growing much, much taller.

It was as if General Dithering's comments had been overheard by the building trades; while homes had become larger and larger over the years, the eight foot ceiling was still reasonably standard throughout the world. Now, home builders and developers were suddenly faced with the prospect of regularly installing ten foot doorways and twelve foot ceilings, to accommodate the plethora of tall homebuyers entering the market. And even that wasn't enough; a nine foot tall couple would walk into a home with enlarged ceilings, enter the kitchen, and immediately complain that the kitchen counters were ridiculously low for their needs. Cabinet makers now had to ensure that counters were at least four feet from the floor.

The real estate industry was in turmoil; tall people began suing builders for discrimination if they continued to build to the old standards, short people felt obliged to sue them if they built to the new standards, and the builders felt as if they were caught right in the middle. And home design wasn't the only problem. There was a veritable cascade of issues coming about.

Bed manufacturers had to establish new sizes to accommodate "the Tallers," as some people began referring to them. This, of course, also had a measurable effect on the bedsheet manufacturers, the latex suppliers, and even the people who made the "do not remove this tag" tags; everything was getting bigger.

It goes without saying that the clothing companies were in an absolute tizzy, but we'll say it anyway; what was once considered Extra Tall was now a medium for the Tallers, while the Shorters (which is how the newly tall now referred rather disparagingly to those who remained with their original statures) still required the traditional sizes. With all this stress, several clothing company executives were seen to be visiting a hair restoration clinic.

The world economy was in a lather; the Tallers, or at least those who had the resources, represented a sudden and significant new demand for housing and a broad range of other goods, while the suppliers had no idea why this was happening, or where it would end. It was rumored that a number of industry executives were so overwrought by the changes, they had to be sent to convalescent homes, which, conveniently enough, tended to be situated near major beach resorts.

In the midst of all this madness, a series of internal and inter-industry meetings ensued to discuss the serious issues facing so many suppliers and manufacturers. At a secret meeting of a major labor organization related to the automobile industry, Hardwick Pounderton addressed the board members. As you may know, Pounderton is the Managing Director of the recently combined International Technicians Society and Union of Recognized Foreign AUtomotive League Technicians; I'm sure you've all seen this organization referred to by its acronym, 'ITSURFAULT.' The worldwide auto industry relied heavily on the membership for manufacturing and technical guidance.

"Ladies and gentlemen, we may have a real issue on our hands. It appears that portions of the customer base are getting taller and taller, and as a result, the market for existing, standard-sized automobiles has seemingly disappeared! While I realize this is a substantial technical opportunity for us going forward, it means recalibrating and re-establishing entire manufacturing lines to a whole new set of parameters, targeting eight and nine foot tall people! I think you can understand the expense involved in such a reconfiguration. We need to ensure that the auto manufacturers pony up the extra funds to support the work, and to retrain the workers. This is going to mean a lot of overtime."

Howard Rashley, one of the board members, and owner of a national chain of auto dealerships, was the first to react. "I don't see the problem, Pounderton; can't they just move the seats back? I realize these people are somewhat taller than your run-of-the-mill tall person, but I can't see this as a big deal. In the worst case, if buyers don't have the headroom, we just put a bubble over the sunroof, call it a 'headroom extension,' and these tall characters can stick their heads into the bubble. It should even offer a kind of futuristic look!" Rashley laughed at his own comment. The rest of the board just smiled nervously.

Pounderton was not amused. "Bubble. Over the sunroof. Right. Rashley, let's get serious here, we're not talking about making a Jetsons cartoon. In order for these people, I've heard them referred to as 'Tallers,' in order for these Tallers to move the seat back enough to drive, the automakers would, at the very least, need to extend the seat rails. If they do that, there won't be any back seat room left! And if we recommend the rail extension, we'll never hear the end of it from the big brass at the major auto companies."

Rashley was ready with a response, unreasonable though it may have been. "Well, if that's the case, they can put a 'GT' on the back of the vehicle, and call it a luxury tourer. We've been selling vehicles with minimal back seats that way for years."

A disturbing murmur passed around the board table as Miriam Reasoner, one of the more senior board members, chimed in.

"Gentlemen, this discussion will get us nowhere. We need to form committees to gather additional information so we know what we're dealing with here. Is this height change here to stay? What's bringing it about? How tall are these people going to get? And why have sales on the current crop of conventional vehicles dropped so precipitously?"

Pounderton listened attentively. "I think I have some insight into that last question, Miriam. Our intelligence indicates that people are hesitant to buy because no one has figured out yet exactly why everyone is getting taller. They could be next, and they don't want to buy a vehicle designated for Shorters if they're going to end up being a Taller by next quarter! I think you're on the right track with that committee idea; let's get some additional information rather than make any rash decisions."

7

"Mr. President, I think it's time we made an announcement to the public." General Dithering was sitting in the Oval Office of The White House, speaking with President Hemminhough, who wore a look of studied concern. No matter what facial expression the President wore, he always seemed to be posing for somebody.

President Markam Hemminhough had succeeded in the last election primarily because (a) he was exceedingly tall and good-looking, (b) he had highly desirable dimples and a cleft chin, which, as everybody knows, are vitally important attributes for any governmental leader, (c) he had a homey way of expressing himself, and (d) he had adopted both a dog and a cat, so he had broad appeal to multiple constituencies. As for his governance, the public perceived him as a man who didn't make too many serious mistakes, and that was good enough for them.

"I don't know, Dithering, we don't want to cause the folks to fly into a panic, now, do we? Before everyone goes off the deep end, let's get some restrictions on this Biepal stuff, if you're sure that's the source of the problem, and see if we can get a handle on this height business from another angle. I'm sure the pharmaceutical companies are looking into remedies already. You know how good they are at responding to the needs of the public in any sort of a medical crisis. You really have to admire their sense of civic responsibility, and especially their longstanding motto: 'Where there's crisis, there's profit.'"

"Mr. President, I believe, from the calls you're receiving, that the public is already off the deep end. We need to take action and get this under control, and soon."

"I'll tell you, Dithering, I'm not sure what all this bother is about. I'm six foot five, and perfectly happy being tall. You'd think people would welcome the opportunity for a little extra height!"

General Dithering was feeling quite agitated at this point. "Well, Mr. President, six foot five is one thing; nine foot five is quite another. And we don't know the limits of this growth yet."

"All right, all right Dithering, don't get your hairpiece in a knot." Dithering briefly displayed an expression of serious annoyance; he was very sensitive about his hair ever since his wife jokingly called him 'baldy' the previous week. But he tried his best to remain focused on the President's continuing commentary. "I should be able to issue an executive order temporarily restricting Biepal sales, assuming I don't get another argument from that blasted Congress, but you know what happens every time we try to control something that the public enjoys; I suspect there's going to be an underground market for this stuff almost immediately, and it's going to be like herding those darned cats trying to get it under control. From what I saw in your report, we don't even know how the stuff is getting into the retail channels!"

It was Dithering's turn to look concerned. "I understand, Mr. President. I think the executive order is at least a good start."

Thanks to informational leaks to various government officials, and many, many disturbing calls to the offices of Senators and Representatives, the U.S. Congress was already engaged in hearings on the issue long before President Hemminhough could issue the order. Several of the more conservative members of Congress were actually considering a national ban on Biepal, while others were recommending a more nuanced approach, and had asked the Food and Drug Administration to form a committee and look into the matter.

Just to complicate matters, six Members of Congress were seriously delaying any progress on the issue because they kept postponing their appearance at the hearings; when they finally arrived on the floor of the House of Representatives, they were seen to be over eight feet tall. This brought about a great deal of ridicule and condemnation from their fellow Congress-people, who immediately began referring to them as the 'Taller Caucus.' The office staff of the Taller Caucus members of course denied that their Representatives had engaged in the use of Biepal, attributing their new-found height to "extra vitamins and special stretching exercises."

President Hemminhough proceeded to issue the executive order, restricting the use of Biepal to 'medical use and scientific experiments,' but the Taller Caucus was instantly opposed to this intervention. At the same time, there was an uproar from a disparate group of constituencies:

The liquor store owners started screaming about restriction of trade, and the substantial impact such an order would have on their sales and profits.

The people who were actually enjoying Biepal staged a demonstration on the grounds of the Capitol building, sporting signs involving words like 'freedom' and 'liberty,' as well as slogans along the lines of 'Heed the Call; Let's be Tall.'"

Another small group of Congress-people, who began calling themselves the 'Biepal Bunch,' formed an alliance with the Taller Caucus, and spoke in strong tones about government overreach, and the fact that no one had actually proven the linkage between Biepal and 'this tallness issue.' They began preparing a bill, to be presented to the Congress for a vote, to override the executive order on Biepal use.

Everyone was arguing with everyone else. In other words, government business was progressing as usual. The Congress did, however, ultimately manage to override the executive order, and so, for the time being, Biepal sales continued unabated.

Members of the academic and business communities couldn't help but take notice of all this Biepal discussion. The whole tallness issue was activating the two strongest motivators for these groups: curiosity and profits.

When President Hemminhough made that comment about the pharmaceutical companies, he knew exactly what he was talking about. While government officials thrashed about in various directions, trying to address the impossible task of keeping all of their various constituents happy, several pharmaceutical companies began to work immediately, in collaboration with major universities, to address the problem, even if they weren't quite sure what the problem was yet, or if it was even a problem at all. But if there was one thing these companies were good at, it was convincing the world that there was a new problem so that they could provide a new solution.

One company in particular, Extrilax Pharmaceuticals, was the first to license a possible molecule recently discovered at a renowned university laboratory in Massachusetts, where scientists had been working on a new formulation that would alter certain growth factors; their goal was to create extremely tall chickens. The driving concept was a chicken leg that would feed a family of four. Extrilax used this formulation as a starting point, and proceeded with the delicate and complicated process of developing a useful vaccine that might counteract the growth drivers in Biepal.

At the same time, the US was collaborating with European authorities to get to the bottom of the whole Biepal business. Various agents had been tracking the substance, and, from what they discovered, they concluded that it may have first appeared somewhere in the United Kingdom.

While the European authorities were certainly concerned, they didn't seem quite as frantic as their US counterparts. General Spendfreeley, a senior figure at NATO Headquarters, was given the task of investigating the issue. Was this

Biepal some variant on an existing drug of some sort? Was it some kind of new secret weapon? Where was it coming from? It was General Spendfreeley's job to find out.

Brigadier General Horace Spendfreeley was a man who had seen somewhere between 50 and 60 planetary revolutions about that star to which we so often refer as The Sun. He was at one time a tall, thin fellow, with spikey hair, bushy eyebrows and a strong jawline. The tall part was still intact, as was the jawline. As for the other attributes, the general had traded in the 'thin' aspect in exchange for a generous quantity of rich foods over the years. The spikey hair had also, for the most part, made a departure for points unknown, leaving a rather shiny pate in its stead. At least the eyebrows were still bushy, although, in proximity to his current baldness, they now had a certain resemblance to two large and furry caterpillars.

We join him as he's discussing the matter with his staff.

"I say, I really don't see what all the fuss is about. Yes, I agree that this Biepal stuff appears to be making some people taller. On the other hand, our Dutch associates, who tend to be on the tall side to begin with, tell me it's having virtually no effect there. And the other countries are reporting that their population is hardly getting any taller than the Dutch were in the first place!"

One of the General's key aides, Colonel Harden, felt obliged to speak up. "Well, General, that may be the case, sir, but we have no idea how much taller the population is going to get. And if this is some kind of newfangled weapon, we really need to be on top of this. My staff has already started preliminary work on a counter-weapon that makes people wider."

The general looked at his aide for a long moment. "I think we're jumping the gun here, Colonel. The first thing we need to do is find out where this Biepal is coming from. Get your people working on it, and come back within the next 48 hours with a preliminary report."

8

"Well, Colonel, what have you found out on that Biepal issue?" Colonel Harden was in General Spendfreeley's office with a preliminary report on the source and characteristics of this new and extraordinary substance.

"You won't believe it, General; you simply won't believe it. I think you'd better see this first, sir." Colonel Harden opened a laptop, and pressed a button. A video started playing.

The general was intrigued, and somewhat confused. "What exactly am I looking at, Colonel?"

"General, this is a video capture from a security camera in a bottle store in Hoboken, New Jersey, a town in the New York area of the United States of America; the U.S. military authorities were good enough to share it with us, after a great deal of coaxing and cajoling. Note the local time is about 0400 when the action on this video took place. The clarity isn't great, but it's good enough to be interesting."

The general stared at the screen for some moments. "Uh, Colonel, I don't seem to be seeing any action here at all."

"Give it a minute, sir; the action begins around time stamp 04:04:11."

The general continued watching the screen. Suddenly, something very odd appeared in a far corner of the room; it seemed like a hole had opened in the wall, but there wasn't any evidence of debris from an explosion, or anything of that sort.

The general's eyes remained glued to the screen, although we should clarify that his eyes actually remained firmly ensconced in his head, where they belonged, and made no actual contact whatsoever with the screen. This is unlike the visual organs of the extraordinarily nearsighted Zepatis Wickatoo creature of Pleebus, a rather friendly mouse-like being with eyes that reside on long stalks, and a popular pet among the Pleebusites. The Zepatis Wickatoo places one or more of its six eyeballs directly on a surface that it wishes to examine. This tends to bring a whole new meaning to the common expression among friends, "stay in touch." We should note that the Pleebusites find this to be quite an endearing characteristic. But let's get back to the video.

Of a sudden, what appeared to be an odd-looking Great Dane walked out of the hole, deposited four boxes using some extra arms it seemed to have at its sides, and returned through the hole. The hole then slowly closed up and completely disappeared, leaving the premises exactly as they had been before this event. The video was completely quiet after that.

"What in the name of Hades did I just see, Colonel?!" The general couldn't believe his eyes. "Is this some sort of hoax? I could swear that a large dog with some extra arms just delivered some boxes to this store, and did it by climbing through a hole in the air!"

"Well, General, I think that pretty well sums it up, sir. We haven't been able to come up with any reasonable explanation for what we've seen."

The general sat back in his chair, staring at a far wall in thought. "Do you think it's a fake? From what we've been discussing about the artificial intelligence threat, I could picture someone fabricating this video to throw us off the trail."

"We considered that, General; the video has been examined by our experts, and they're quite confident that it's genuine. Unfortunately, that doesn't get us any closer to an explanation as to how a big, strange dog shows up from absolutely nowhere to deliver boxes to a bottle shop in the middle of the night." They sat contemplating the issue in silence; a full two minutes passed before the colonel remembered something.

"We did get one outlandish idea, from one of my lieutenants, who happens to be a big sci-fi fan. But I'm afraid you'll think it's crazy, sir."

"Colonel, at this point, I have an open mind on the subject. We obviously can't report what we've just seen to, well, anyone! They'll think that we've completely lost our minds! As for your idea, go ahead; try me."

Well, sir, Lieutenant Snerdel thought that perhaps the hole we saw appear suddenly in the store was some sort of a spatial rift. The dog creature could therefore be an alien being."

The general just sat there looking at the colonel for a few moments. "A spatial rift... and an alien. Uh huh. I see."

"I did warn you that it was a crazy idea."

"Great, so now we're chasing aliens." The General considered the explanation for a moment longer, wearing an expression of disbelief. He threw up his hands. "Well, Colonel, we don't have anything else to work with; we may as well pursue the 'crazy' until we have something sane to work on. See if you can get any further confirmation on this video; are there any other videos of this ilk that we can find? Any other reports of such incidents? In the meantime, I'll make inquiries with my counterparts across the continent, as well as our contacts in the United Kingdom; those fellows in the United States seem to think that this Biepal first appeared somewhere in Britain." The general looked pensive for a moment. "Ah, if it had only been some new form of tea instead. Oh well; let's reconvene by week's end, and compare notes."

Colonel Harden was back in General Spendfreeley's office two days later, confirming the sighting of large dogs delivering boxes of Biepal, through holes formed seemingly in the middle of the air. "General, we've gathered three additional surveillance videos showing basically the same thing we saw earlier. Our people simply have no explanation for what we're looking at."

"Well that's just marvelous, Colonel, just fantastic. I have the European administrators here in Brussels on my back, the Americans seem to be going quite mad over the repercussions of this tallness business, and my wife is ready to send me to either a pet shop or to Denmark, because she says I keep muttering something about Great Danes in my sleep. What am I supposed to report to my superiors? That we're seeing large dogs selling an unusual form of beverage?! I'd be reassigned to an arctic outpost before I have time to buy a parka!"

The general wasn't thrilled, and couldn't help continuing his rant. "I've been doing some homework of my own, Colonel. It seems there was a lightly reported incident several months ago that might have some bearing on this case. I have the report right here." The General shuffled through a pile of papers on his desk, found the report in question, and began perusing the file as he continued speaking.

"It took place somewhere in the Yorkshire area of England, I believe. I was informed that it was filed under 'far-fetched' apparently for two primary reasons: first, the military participants involved were something less than the, ahem, brightest bulbs in the proverbial chandelier, if you catch my meaning." The Colonel nodded knowingly.

"The second reason it was considered far-fetched is far more interesting, from the perspective of our current dilemma. Apparently, a member of the local armed forces reported quashing what he considered to be a potential, and I place this in the most substantial quotes I can manage, 'alien invasion' in the middle of some woman's living room. This fellow, a Sergeant Major Greene, managed to blow up a good portion of the woman's kitchen, as well as, dare I read it out loud, certain notable potted plants." Both gentlemen cringed.

The General suddenly spoke in quiet tones. "Curiously enough, after one wades through what appears to be this utter nonsense, there's a description in the report that seems to coincide rather remarkably with that hole formation we saw on the video feed." Both men were silent for a moment as they considered the implications. "Greene's story was rather heavily discounted, and, according to this report, he was sent off to some far-flung exchange post in Canada to get his act together. I made some inquiries, and Greene returned to a desk job in the United Kingdom about a month ago."

"As crazy as his story sounds, he's the only one of us with earlier experience that coincides with what we've been seeing here with respect to this Biepal business. I say we hand this off to the locals in Yorkshire, and let this Greene fellow investigate it further. Thoughts, Colonel?"

The Colonel nodded and smiled. "General, I think that's a first-class idea." After working with the General for some time, it had become clear to the Colonel that General Spendfreeley had a certain expertise in transferring to others the responsibility for annoying tasks.

Within hours, a communiqué from Brigadier General Spendfreeley was received in the offices of Colonel Reginald Messington, commanding the North Yorkshire Regiment. Messington was in the middle of a weekly staff meeting when a messenger rushed in with a sealed envelope, marked 'Urgent.' Messington felt obliged to interrupt the meeting and determine what it was that was so "bloody important." He read it over. Twice.

"Ladies and gentlemen, I've been informed that, apparently, there are some unusual goings-on in both Europe and the United States that, oddly enough, may have originated in our jurisdiction. As much as I would like to assign one of you to investigate it further, I have most unfortunately been instructed to assign a particular officer to the task."

His junior officers look at him in horror. "Oh, no...! No, sir, you can't mean..."

9

Sergeant Major DeLade Greene was in a good mood as he drove through the Yorkshire countryside, and proceeded to the village of Hampsthwaite. He progressed along a series of picturesque lanes, with views that practically defined the term 'pastoral,' until he came upon a small cottage, with what appeared to be a relatively new conservatory protruding from the back of the dwelling.

Sergeant Major Greene didn't think twice about parking his very heavy, very military-looking vehicle on the front lawn of the residence. He then proceeded to the front entrance, where he made generous use of the knocker, which distinctly resembled a sheep, positioned in the middle of the door. He had essentially forgotten about the platoon of heavily armed soldiers following behind him in a large truck, ready to pounce at his command. They followed his example, and parked their extremely heavy truck similarly. It was not a good day for the Hensworthy lawn.

As soon as Mrs. Hensworthy opened the door, and before she could issue forth a single word, or so much as a gasp, Sergeant Major Greene started speaking rather loudly.

"Ah, madam, I am Sergeant Major DeLade Greene of the North Yorkshire Regiment. You may recall my previous visit, when I successfully squashed a potential alien invasion before the beasties could wreak their so-called 'havoc' on our world. Haha! Lucky, that; indeed, indeed!" Sergeant Major Greene had placed the word "havoc" rather notably in quotes. He proceeded to march past Mrs. Hensworthy into her living room as he continued his diatribe.

"You may thank me again later, madam. For the present, I have been informed that certain, shall we say, creatures of an unusual sort have been detected in places where such creatures do not belong. No, no, no, they do not belong at all!" He lowered his voice considerably as he continued. "I have been entrusted with this vitally important absolutely top top secret mission, and I shan't tell you more, madam, as it's all quite classified, oh yes, very hush hush, woosh woosh, and all that sort, and the walls may very well have ears, if you get my drift. Haha!"

The Sergeant Major then resumed his rather bellowing tone. "Since beasties of an alien sort were found here before, my superiors thought this to be a logical starting point to investigate this new little problem. And with, in all modesty, my extensive experience with this sort of thing, I was the logical choice to investigate this new potential, shall we say, infestation." Mrs. Hensworthy noted about twelve bored-looking soldiers, variously sitting, squatting, or otherwise reclining on her front lawn, visible beyond the doorway. They didn't seem the least bit interested in the proceedings.

The Sergeant Major wasn't quite through yet. "And who, madam, may I ask, is this gentleman residing in your living room? Who, indeed? Another alien, perhaps?" The Sergeant Major was seen to noticeably smirk.

Mrs. Hensworthy looked extremely annoyed at this intrusion. "Are you *quite* through, Sergeant Major? I remember you all too well, I assure you, as you're the utter fool who, upon your previous visit, not only destroyed my kitchen, but completely obliterated Maurice!"

Upon hearing this, Sergeant Major Greene wore a somewhat shocked expression. "Maurice? Maurice?! I don't recall any casualties on our last encounter. This should have been reported to us at once! At once, I say!"

Before he could continue, Mrs. Hensworthy interjected. "Sergeant Major, Maurice was my favorite philodendron plant. And if you must know, this is my husband, Malthorp, thank you very much. Why in the world are you back here? Weren't you rightfully sent off to some extraordinarily desolate and frigid wilderness for all the nonsense you brought about here the last time?"

"And all this talk of an alien invasion. I can assure you that any visitors I care to entertain in my living room have no desire to invade anything more than my tea cupboard and collection of desserts! Alien invasion... the very idea!"

As Mrs. Hensworthy spoke, Sergeant Major Greene was seen to be sniffing around her living room, paying particular attention to the doorway through her bookcase, connecting to the kitchen.

"Come, come now, madam, I am well aware of the unusual goings-on here. We both know you had some very odd beings in this very room upon my previous interjection, this very room, I say, and it's a good thing I was here! Oh, yes, oh yes, oh yes indeed! Without my lads having properly closed up that portal sort of thingamabob I clearly observed in this very room, that portal that must have led to heaven-knows-what sort of devious and devilish alien worlds, we might very well have been overrun by all sorts of beasties, munching on our very flesh! Yes, munching, I say! So let's have none of your indignation, madam!"

The Sergeant Major tried to adopt a conciliatory tone. "Why don't you save us a great deal of trouble, madam, and simply show us how these new infiltrators, if I may call them that, are making their appearance once again, and we'll clear up the issue straight-away. Yes, straight-away."

Mrs. Hensworthy's face now approximated the color of a ripe tomato as her annoyance with Sergeant Major DeLade Greene experienced a particularly notable crescendo. She did her best to maintain her composure as she spoke. "Sergeant Major, I can see I will need to have words once again with my friend Colonel Messington. Why don't I give him a call, and perhaps we can resolve this little matter satisfactorily." She finished the sentence through gritted teeth as she reached for her phone, and began searching her contacts.

10

"Mrs. Hensworthy, I'm afraid I really do need to ask for your cooperation this time." Several days had passed since Sergeant Major DeLade Greene visited the Hensworthy residence, and Mrs. Hensworthy was now sitting in Colonel Messington's office as he tried to convince her to be helpful in his investigation.

"We have some very strange goings-on, umm, going on, and they bear a striking resemblance to the activities reported earlier in your very living room by the Sergeant Major." Mrs. Hensworthy scoffed rather noticeably. The Colonel chose to ignore her scoff, and continued.

"I'm going to show you a video I received recently from a senior officer at NATO headquarters. It's to be considered highly confidential; you mustn't discuss this with anyone." Colonel Messington hit a button on his computer keyboard, and a large screen on his office wall sprang to life. A few moments later, even though the image was a bit grainy, Mrs.

Hensworthy could clearly discern the signs of an interdimensional rift establishing itself in what appeared to be the corner of a bottle store; a Kinglorf stepping carefully through the rift and depositing several boxes on the floor of the store; and the same said Kinglorf then carefully returning through the rift. The rift then closed behind the creature, disappearing completely.

"Well, Mrs. Hensworthy, do you have any insights on what we've just observed?"

Mrs. Hensworthy took a moment to gather her thoughts. "Colonel, if I had wanted to see a low budget Halloween movie, I'm sure I could find several on the various underwhelming and overpriced pay channels currently available on my television. What, exactly, was I supposed to be observing, pray tell?"

The Colonel felt a bit exasperated. "Oh, please, Mrs. Hensworthy, do be serious! That whirling opening we just observed in the middle of, well, *nothing*, is exactly the sort of opening described by Sergeant Major Greene when he attended to what he called..." the Colonel turned to consult a file on his desk containing some notes... "an 'alien infestation' in your living room! Now, that simply can't be a coincidence! So why don't you tell us what you know about this latest incident we just observed in the video, hmm?"

"Colonel, for all I know, Sergeant Major DeLade Greene had this video created simply to bolster his credibility and get himself promoted to some position with a shorter title. Heaven knows having to say 'sergeant major' all the time must be terribly tiring. If you'd like to provide me with a copy of this video, I'll be happy to show it around the neighborhood and see if anyone has anything worthwhile to add to the discussion. Otherwise, I believe we're done here."

"As I mentioned earlier, Mrs. Hensworthy, that video is quite, quite confidential, and so I won't be able to provide you with a copy." The Colonel wore a look of substantial disappointment; he didn't actually sigh, but from the look on his face, you could swear he did. "If you're going to take that attitude, I suppose we're not going to get any further today. But mark my words, madam, we have our eyes on you! And the Sergeant Major will be keeping a keen eye on your neighborhood and abode. Any unusual visitors, and we're going to know about it, believe you me! Good day to you, madam!"

Mrs. Hensworthy made a hasty retreat, and proceeded to return home as quickly as possible. As she pulled into the drive, she noticed a somewhat dilapidated service truck parked across the lane, marked *Suck-It-Up Vacuum Cleaner Repair; we'll come back 'til you can vac*. She rushed into the house.

Malthorp was in his customary spot in the living room, enjoying a little reading and a cup of tea. He looked up as Mrs. Hensworthy rushed through the door and hurriedly closed it behind her. "Ah, Eleanora my dear, welcome back; how was your visit with Colonel Messington?"

"Malthorp, please help me close the drapes! I believe they have us under surveillance!"

Malthorp did his best to look concerned. "Who might that be, my dear?"

"Why, the military, Malthorp, the *military*! They're hoping to catch a glimpse of an interdimensional rift! I'm sure of it. There's an odd truck parked across the lane, and I wouldn't be a bit surprised if it's filled with all sorts of surveillance equipment, eavesdropping gadgets, and goodness knows what sort of widgets these people use to invade other people's space!"

Mrs. Hensworthy proceeded to close all the draperies as Malthorp watched. He displayed his usual level of calm, although he did want to appear empathetic. "Eleanora, aren't we getting just a tad paranoid? I realize that character Greene is quite the annoyance, but do you really think they're taking the trouble to watch us? I would think it's going to be a very boring assignment for them, I must say."

Mrs. Hensworthy peeked carefully through her drapes at the truck as she responded. "You don't understand, Malthorp! Colonel Messington showed me a surveillance video of a Kinglorf stepping through a rift and delivering the goods! *Our* goods!"

"Oh, goodness! I shouldn't even be saying 'Kinglorf' or 'our goods;' they might be listening! Goodness gracious, I've just said them again! Anyway, since that imbecile Greene described seeing a rift in our living room the last time he showed up, they think we have something to do with it!"

Now Malthorp wore a look of genuine concern. "You say he showed you a video? Do you have a copy of the video, by any chance?"

Mrs. Hensworthy continued to stare at the truck across the way as she continued to speak, now in practically whispering tones. "No, they kept telling me everything was confidential, and wouldn't give me a bloody copy!"

Malthorp briefly gave the matter some serious thought. "Well, we'd better get in touch with Mr. Farpel; he needs to know that his cover's been blown, so to speak, although I'm sure the authorities still don't have any idea what they're looking at on that video. But Mr. Farpel clearly needs to be more careful."

"That's just it, Malthorp! We don't have any way to contact him. He always contacts us!"

Malthorp had an idea. "Aren't we getting a payment from the Biepal distributor in the next couple of days? Mr. Farpel knows that schedule;

doesn't he typically show up for his box of carrots shortly thereafter?"

"Yes...yes! We could leave him a note with the carrots!"

"You know, I'm not sure a note is the best idea, Eleanora. First, Mr. Farpel may think the paper is just some sort of carrot wrapping. And second, I'm not sure he's comfortable with our written language at this point. The GadgiYack is a great little invention, but it doesn't translate text yet. I have another thought."

With that, Malthorp headed in the direction of the kitchen, toward the back of the house, and Mrs. Hensworthy heard him open the back door of the solarium, which was just past the kitchen.

Mrs. Hensworthy mumbled to herself, "What is he doing! They might see him going out the back door!" She ran toward the back, but by the time she arrived, Malthorp was once again entering the abode.

"Malthorp! I told you we're under surveillance! They might have seen you go out!"

"So?" Malthorp appeared unperturbed. "I just had to get a little something from my vessel. I closed the door of the garden shed, Eleanora; I'm sure no one saw anything. Do try to relax a bit, my dear."

"It's all so disturbing. What was it in your vessel that was so important, anyway?"

"Just *this*." Malthorp held up a small cylindrical object, about the size of a common flash drive. "It's a holo-recorder, so we can leave a holographic message for Mr. Farpel. I'm sure he'll recognize this device when he sees it. And now I'm more confident we can leave him a message to which he'll actually pay attention."

11

Back in the United States, the public had rather messily divided into the 'Taller' and 'Shorter' constituencies, each pushing its own particular agenda, with a fringe set of Tallers who desired to once again be shorter, and a more substantial group of Shorters who desired to be taller.

For reasons unknown, some Shorters were immune to the effects of Biepal; no matter how much they indulged, they just remained short. The experts surmised it had something to do with their particular genes. Needless to say, this group wanted the government to develop a treatment so that they too could "reach to new heights," as the group's representatives so eloquently expressed it.

Extrilax Pharmaceuticals, who, as we mentioned earlier, was working on a vaccine to counter the effects of Biepal, had come up with several variations of a possible inoculation that would interrupt the growth aspect; they proceeded to initiate limited clinical trials. There were some noteworthy side effects.

Observing the clinical trial sites, journalists followed a small group of subjects testing Variation A of the vaccine. The subjects entered the trial at over 9 feet tall, but were seen to be 2.5 to 3 feet tall within six weeks of initiating treatment. While Extrilax considered this to be a resounding success, the company did admit that the vaccine rather overshot the mark, so to speak. To minimize public ridicule, Extrilax was good enough to provide chauffeurs for the test subjects, as they were no longer tall enough to reach the pedals in their vehicles. Each subject also received a free Extrilax lollipop.

Another group of subjects, who represented a slightly shorter 8 foot category of Biepal users, tested Variation B of the vaccine. Some two weeks after initiating the trial, the test subjects were seen to emerge from the testing facility covered head to toe in long purple fur; unfortunately, they also appeared to remain approximately 8 feet tall. This resulted in various erroneous 'Bigfoot' sightings in the vicinity of the trial site. On the bright side, no chauffeurs were required for this group.

Marilyn Slickton, spokesperson for Extrilax Pharmaceuticals, issued a statement clarifying that "there may be some rare side effects from these medications, but the data indicate that, all in all, they are perfectly safe for human use." When asked about the unusual trial results, Ms. Slickton suggested that the press review the trial data themselves, and assured them that the data would absolutely without a doubt be available sometime within the next century.

It's worth noting that Ms. Slickton was subsequently seen at the local pharmacy, buying up all the packages of safety razors and a great deal of shaving cream. And the search continued for a viable vaccine.

While all this was transpiring, there was a small panic that occurred when an unusual news story spread across the internet. Apparently, a reporter from Watt Snew Terribly Reliable Honest News Media, Inc. quoted from what they claimed to be a reliable source that "Biepal is actually People! It's made from People! Why do you think it rhymes so perfectly?! It's cannibalism, I tell you!" The panic quickly subsided when a well-known forensic laboratory confirmed that Biepal is "a fermented fruit juice, probably from some sort of berry." Watt Snew News quickly retracted the article, claiming one of their employees "let her kid play with our news feed."

Meanwhile, at the Pentagon, in the secret offices of TEXTING, General Dithering had some new concerns. His aide Colonel Crassik was discussing it with him.

"General, we're getting some disturbing reports from our agents overseas, sir. It appears that certain former Eastern Bloc countries, as well as several countries in the Far East, are providing their troops with Biepal, in an effort to secure the tallest forces in the world. We also have reports that these same countries are trying to derive a serum from Biepal, so that the troops don't actually need to drink the beverage in order to get the effects in an accelerated manner."

The General was not happy at this news. "Colonel, how are they even *getting* this stuff?! And on the subject of troops, everyone knows we have the best of the best of the best troops on the planet, and we need to keep it that way, by gum! I believe we'll need to present this to the Joint Chiefs of Staff, but if those Rooskies and Chinese types want to play it this way, we'll need to beat them at this game and get that Biepal into our own troops!"

The Colonel was quiet for a moment. "Yes, General, I understand the concern. We're still working on the supply chain question, sir. As for plying our troops with Biepal, don't you think it might be advisable to understand what is actually happening with this beverage with respect to the height issue; determine the possible side effects; and so forth, before we jump into the unknown?"

The General spoke with authority. "No time, man, no time! If those other countries are moving on this, we need to get on top of it as soon as possible! You know my motto, Colonel, 'Ready, Fire, Aim!'"

The Colonel thought that adhering to such a motto would lead to a great deal of unnecessary and unfortunate damage, but in the interests of diplomacy, he kept his thoughts to himself.

Within six weeks, the U.S. military was providing Biepal to a select group of special forces. In order to acquire the beverage without attracting too much attention, the Army was given the responsibility of forming a special corps, comprised of 100 carefully selected little old ladies, to be known as the Biepal Team. A group of renowned psychologists created a detailed list of criteria for choosing these women, foremost of which was a specially derived and highly confidential 'blend-into-the-crowd' factor, known as *Factor B_c*: a set of physical characteristics that would virtually ensure no one would notice these women as they bought up substantial quantities of Biepal at their local liquor stores.

Four weeks later, after initiating the application of Biepal to the troops, Colonel Crassik was back in General Dithering's office with more disturbing news.

"General, we have an unanticipated side effect that I believe is going to bring *Operation Biepal* to a premature end, sir."

"What now, Colonel?! Are the troops getting taller or aren't they?"

"Well, General, it's still a bit early in the Biepal cycle to determine how much height our troops will gain. The bigger problem, sir, is that those indulging in Biepal have lost all interest in the military; they've become complete pacifists. A number of the troops have been observed walking around the base trying to protect lady bugs, spiders, and other such creatures around their barracks, and they refuse to engage in gunnery practice because, and I quote, they 'might damage those nicely painted target boards.' It's frankly somewhat embarrassing."

The General sat with his elbows on the desk, his hands covering his face. "That's just swell, Colonel."

"Uh, there's one other thing that I'm loathe to mention, General. The troops have also developed an insatiable craving...." The Colonel hesitated for a moment.

The General looked up. "Craving? Craving for what, exactly? What exactly is it they crave, Colonel?"

The Colonel noticeably cringed. "Broadway musicals, sir." He paused for another moment.

"Uh, specifically, *The Sound of Music*, and *Hello, Dolly!*. They've been screening them now each evening for the past week."

The General wore a look of horror as he contemplated the implications. His countenance then assumed a look of resignation as he responded in quite an exasperated tone. "All right, Colonel, I suppose we'll need to bring *Operation Biepal* to a close. Have the news hounds gotten wind of any of this yet?"

"No, General, we've managed to keep it under wraps; security has been tight on this, sir."

"Thank goodness for that! We don't need those blasted reporters telling the world that our troops prefer Broadway musicals to battle plans! And you may as well disband the Biepal Team. The only consolation I can see here is that our adversaries must be facing the same problems!"

12

Dearlotin Farpelmop was feeling somewhat disturbed. He wasn't accustomed to this feeling, as he usually had everything under control. He was standing in the Hensworthy's living room in response to a holo-message he found the previous night, when he dropped in to retrieve his payment of carrots in exchange for Biepal deliveries.

"How? How could this have happened? I must be getting careless, and that ain't good. It's probably from hanging out with that Kolameas Elwinkem; she's making my brain cells wither." As for the carelessness comment, he was referring to Colonel Messington's video, that captured one of his hench-Kinglorfs delivering boxes of Biepal to a bottle shop. Mrs. Hensworthy had filled him in on all the recent activities, including the visit from the 'beloved' Sergeant Major Greene.

Malthorp was the first to chime in. "Well, Mr. Farpel, let us not dwell on that. The real question is, where do we go from here? Mrs. Hensworthy and I are living like virtual prisoners with that vacuum cleaner repair truck parked outside our home, observing our every move, and I think it's only a matter of time before some authority or other figures out exactly what it is they're seeing on that video. I would say it would probably be to our distinct advantage to avoid an alien-related panic for the moment."

Farpel considered the issue briefly in silence. "Well, if you like, I can arrange to open an interdimensional rift beneath that truck outside, and transition it to another 3-space where it won't do any harm. I should say that would slow down their surveillance activity quite a bit." Farpel smirked noticeably.

Mrs. Hensworthy wasn't keen on that idea; her sarcasm meter went completely off the scale. "Oh, yes, Mr. Farpel, I'm sure that would be just fine, having a truck disappear into thin air through a hole, that also suddenly appears out of thin air and disappears the same way. You don't think anyone might notice, do you? Just having a truck evaporate that way?"

Detecting sarcasm wasn't necessarily Farpel's strongest suit. "Well, I wouldn't do it during the *daytime*." Mrs. Hensworthy just shook her head back and forth.

Farpel gave the issue some additional thought. "Can we review the video? Maybe the issue isn't as bad as you think."

Mrs. Hensworthy was struggling to maintain her composure. "That bloody Colonel Messington wouldn't give it to me! He kept waving the confidentiality flag in my face. Say, Mr. Farpel, perhaps you could just drop in on Colonel Messington's office, perhaps when no one is home, so to speak, and pick up that video yourself! Maybe if we have a chance to review it in detail, it will give us some additional ideas as to what we might do."

As a Kinglorf of action, Farpel was always in favor of moving forward, whatever that happened to mean at the time. "Not a problem, lady. Just tell me what I'm looking for, and where I'm going, and I'll have it here in a Whicket Minute!"

As a reminder for those who may have forgotten their astro-geography, the planet Whicket 2, the second of twelve planets in the Whicket system, rotates 360 degrees about its axis in approximately 12 Earth minutes, and revolves around its star in 2.4 Earth days. As we may have mentioned before, it isn't a terribly productive planet, as the inhabitants spend most of their time attending birthday parties. According to the clocks on Whicket 2, a Whicket Minute would last approximately 0.132 Earth seconds, which is a very short time indeed. But let's get back to our story.

That night, as Malthorp and Mrs. Hensworthy watched with interest, Farpel inflated his extremely handy flotation pouches, rose back to their living room ceiling, proceeded through the interdimensional rift that still resided there, and onward into a darkened space that the Hensworthys could not quite discern.

Farpel proceeded to quite literally drop in on Colonel Messington's office through another interdimensional rift he had created in the good Colonel's office ceiling (after all, his favorite form of arrival); it's worth noting that it barely took him any time at all to move from the Hensworthy living room to the Colonel's office; with Farpel's expertise in dimensional folding, he folded the discrete 3-space residing between the rifts in such a way that he essentially joined the Hensworthy's ceiling to that of the office, and stepped through the opening.

He then began looking for a small red flash drive; Mrs. Hensworthy had given Farpel a detailed description of the device, as otherwise, Farpel might have no idea what a flash drive actually looked like. She also noted that the drive might be locked in a cabinet or desk.

Kinglorfs have excellent night vision, and so Farpel was able to look around without turning on any lights. He saw nothing that resembled the flash drive. He mumbled to himself as he gave the matter some thought.

"Well, it certainly ain't obvious. I hope Mrs. Hensworthy got the description right. I guess I'll need to transcend some of these 3-dimensional obstacles here to see if it's residing out of my current line of sight." Under ordinary circumstances, 'transcending these 3-dimensional obstacles' would mean breaking into the desk and filing cabinets. With Farpel's particular skills, however, he was able to avoid such crudity.

Farpel proceeded to open another interdimensional rift and transition into a different 3-space. From that vantage point, he opened various interdimensional micro-rifts from his current locale and into the desk drawers, file drawers, a storage cabinet and a floor safe residing in Colonel Messington's office, until he espied the object in question, i.e., the red flash drive containing the video, where it resided on the top shelf of the floor safe. "Ah, easy as taking worbles from a gridnap." As I'm sure you know, that is, in fact, quite an easy thing to do, as worbles tend to be very slippery, and gridnaps don't have a very strong grip. And for those who tend to worry about protecting the furniture (you know the type: coasters everywhere, covers on the comfy seating, etc.), please note that no furniture was harmed in the pursuit of the object in question.

Farpel took possession of the flash drive, and proceeded to close the micro-rifts he had created. He then returned to the 3-space in which the office resided, i.e., the 3-dimensional space with which we humans are so well acquainted; rose back to the ceiling of the office; stepped back through the office ceiling rift; and continued on through the other side of the dimensional fold he had created, namely, the rift that remained in the Hensworthy living room ceiling. This took a total elapsed time of approximately 4.478 minutes.

Mrs. Hensworthy looked up to see Farpel dropping back into the room. "Back so soon, Mr. Farpel? Is there some issue?"

Farpel proceeded to hand her the flash drive. "No issue, lady; here's your flash thingywhatsit. Oh, wow, I can't believe I just said that; I *am* spending too much time with Kolameas Elwinkem!" Farpel winced.

Mrs. Hensworthy was quite astonished. "But, you just left the room a moment ago!"

Farpel smiled. "The advantages of interdimensional transit, lady. If you don't mind, I'd like to take a gander at that video."

Mrs. Hensworthy took the flash drive from Farpel, and proceeded to plug it into a laptop she had on an adjacent side table; she then copied the video to her hard drive. Malthorp and Farpel watched over her shoulder as the screen came to life with the video from the drive.

It was exactly as Mrs. Hensworthy had described it; they watched the rather grainy image as a Kinglorf emerged from a newly formed rift, deposited some boxes, and departed, leaving the locale otherwise unchanged.

All were silent for a moment, until Farpel spoke up. "Well, I can't say much for their video technology. That's a pretty weak image, and it's not even 3-dimensional."

Mrs. Hensworthy looked rather distraught again. "I *know* that, but unfortunately, it still shows a *Kinglorf* stepping through a *rift*! Oh, goodness, I really need to stop saying these things out loud." Mrs. Hensworthy then spoke toward the curtained window rather loudly, "YOU PEOPLE IN THE TRUCK! STOP LISTENING TO ME! STOP IT, I SAY!"

Malthorp put his arm around her. "Now, now, Eleanora, let's not get too excited here. After all, we aren't sure they're even listening to us."

Mrs. Hensworthy did not look consoled, and proceeded to speak in a low voice. "Well, they *might* be, and we don't need to take unnecessary risks!"

While this transpired, Farpel had been thinking about the video. He smiled. "I have an idea how to pull the gridnap's horns, so to speak."

Malthorp and Mrs. Hensworthy just looked at him rather blankly.

Farpel figured he'd better clarify; it was pretty clear that, as a Barnorklet, Mrs. Hensworthy didn't get the reference. And Farpel guessed that Malthorp had simply resided on this particular orb too long. He spoke slowly.

"Oh, wow; *how to remove the potential damage to us from this video*, people!"

Malthorp and Mrs. Hensworthy both smiled rather broadly, but Mrs. Hensworthy became a bit frustrated when Farpel failed to continue. "So? How do we do that?!"

"Look, lady, I can't get into it right now. I'm gonna make a copy of this video data; I have an interesting application in mind." With that, Farpel opened a small satchel he had at his side, and removed what appeared to be a bright purple worm. He held it carefully in his appendage; it squirmed.

While Mrs. Hensworthy was generally quite fond of worms, and the lovely work they did in her garden, she was not terribly excited about having one residing in her living room. And particularly a bright purple one; or one that squirmed.

"Mr. Farpel, what in heaven's name is that?!"

Farpel brought the worm to her laptop, and set it on the keyboard. "Oh, you don't know? This is a Padgenok Dragon from the Kor Planets. It has a handy habit of absorbing ordered electromagnetic structures." As they watched the worm on the keyboard, it suddenly sprouted four beautiful and delicate wings, and the tail grew to an arrowed point. Mrs. Hensworthy gasped.

Farpel explained what they were seeing. "Yeah, it kind of does that when it comes across a rich vein of electromagnetic content. It's absorbing everything from the memory circuits of this thingamabob," referring to the laptop. He suddenly thought about what he just said. "Oh, no! That's it! I definitely need some space from that Elwinkem!"

"Anyway, if I then put it on a memory circuit more or less devoid of ordered electromagnetic content, and squeeze it just behind the wings, it regurgitates all the data into that space."

Malthorp was impressed. "So you're basically performing a data transfer operation using the, what did you call it, a Padgenok Dragon?"

The dragon had retracted its wings, and essentially returned to purple worm form. "There, it's done munching. Yeah, I'm getting the video data this way." Farpel returned the worm to his satchel. "They're really handy to have around, and they don't eat much. A few data sets a week keeps them happy."

Malthorp suddenly had a thought. "Mr. Farpel, perhaps you might return that flash drive to the locale from which you retrieved it earlier. I don't think we really want Colonel Messington to know that someone has absconded with his classified data."

Farpel took possession of the flash drive, and began rising to the ceiling once again. "I had that same thought, actually. I'll replace it right where I found it, and then I'm off. I got stuff I need to do if we're going to defuse this video exposure. Later, Barnork-dwellers!"

With that, Farpel disappeared through the rift in the ceiling, and, as he passed through the dimensional fold and re-entered Colonel Messington's office, the rift opening in the Hensworthy's ceiling slowly closed behind him.

13

A few days later, Mrs. Hensworthy was again feeling rather anxious. That blasted vacuum cleaner repair truck was still parked in the lane outside the cottage, and she hadn't heard anything further from Mr. Farpel.

As a distraction, she decided to turn on the small television she had in the kitchen. She didn't watch often, but there were a few channels she did enjoy. She began watching The Potted Plant Channel, one of the streaming services she found to be particularly exciting.

Mrs. Hensworthy was inevitably annoyed whenever a commercial message interrupted the show she was watching. She happened to be in the middle of a six-part series entitled *The Petunia Plant: A Love Story*, when, as expected, a commercial began to air.

She was about to walk away during the commercial message and prepare a cup of tea, when something on the screen caught her attention. She couldn't believe her eyes; she was seeing the video of the Kinglorf delivering Biepal! She called out promptly. "Malthorp! Please come over here right away! You're not going to believe what I'm seeing here!"

Malthorp rushed into the kitchen, and looked at the screen just as a deep-voiced announcer began speaking over the video feed:

"Have you tried the delicious beverage Biepal? Biepal, delivered nightly to your local shops by special elven messengers from an extraordinary Lost World. Just for your enjoyment!!"

As the video of the Kinglorf came to a close, the screen faded to white. Of a sudden, several amazingly long arms reached in from the edges to the middle of the screen, with elegant drinking glasses in hand, just like on the still-frame ad we showed you earlier, and clinked the glasses, as in a toast; the glasses were filled with a cheery-looking beverage. A bright orange banner then faded in at the top of the image:

"Are you people Biepal People?"

And the commercial came to an end.

Malthorp and Mrs. Hensworthy just looked at each other for several moments. Even the petunias now displayed on the screen couldn't distract them. Malthorp reacted first.

"Huh. I wonder if the inhabitants of Zorbel 4 got paid for that last bit at the end. They certainly do have long arms."

Mrs. Hensworthy couldn't believe it. "*That's* your reaction?! This has to be Mr. Farpel's work! Now everyone will know about the Kinglorfs! How can you just sit there smiling?!"

Malthorp was extremely calm. "Don't you see, Eleanora? Mr. Farpel has rendered this video evidence completely harmless! If Messington or any of the other authorities try to use it as evidence now, everyone will simply assume it was a fantasy created for the commercial, and completely discount it! I have to hand it to Mr. Farpel; a truly brilliant maneuver."

Mrs. Hensworthy took a deep breath. "I never thought of it that way. Amazing! Well, that *is* certainly a relief! But how ever did he air that commercial on television?"

"Well, I suppose we'll just need to ask him when we see him next. In the meantime, suppose we celebrate with a nice cup of tea?"

Meanwhile, in the vacuum cleaner repair truck parked across the lane, Cora Nosely and Malcolm Schlectwetter, two intelligence (and we use the term generously) agents under contract to Colonel Messington, were continuing to carefully monitor the Hensworthy household.

"I just don't know what we're doing here, Malcolm. I've been staring through this annoying vacuum cleaner periscope for days now, and all I see are some closed curtains. As for the audio surveillance, I'm hearing a bunch of squeaks, pops and high-pitched whines. I just don't think the bloody sonic pickup is working right."

"Patience, Cora, patience. Remember, Messington is paying us by the day, so let's milk this as much as we can."

"I get that, Malcolm, but Messington is also going to expect some kind of results for his money. I don't think video images showing draperies or some audio of what appears to be static are going to satisfy him. And if we don't satisfy him, he's not going to keep calling us for these jobs."

Malcolm gave the issue some thought. "Well, Cora, we could do what we did for that surveillance job on the goulash shop Messington suspected of being a safe house for Hungarian spies; substitute in the video from an old 1950's spy movie. He fell for that one pretty easily, although, when everyone figured it out, I imagine the subsequent apology to the Hungarian Government was kind of painful."

"Yeah, Malcolm, I don't think we can get away with that one again."

"We need to give it more time, Cora! These people look like real amateurs; they're *bound* to make a mistake soon."

Back in the Hensworthy house, not more than an Earth hour later, the Hensworthys were enjoying their customary cup of afternoon tea, when a familiar whirling began to make itself evident in the vicinity of their living room ceiling. Moments later, Farpel dropped in for a visit.

This time, Mrs. Hensworthy was ready for an otherworldly conversation; she handed Malthorp a GadgiYack, and positioned her own in a handy nostril.

"Why Mr. Farpel! We were just talking about you. So nice to see you again."

"Yeah, yeah, I wasn't sure if you had seen the video ad for Biepal. If you haven't, I'm here to let you know about it. If you have, I figured you probably have some questions."

Malthorp chimed in. "As a matter of fact, Mr. Farpel, we *have* seen the ad, and I must say, I think you've done a splendid job of defusing that video of a Kinglorf making a Biepal delivery."

Mrs. Hensworthy interrupted hurriedly. "Malthorp, the truck outside! Please be careful what you say!" She then noticed Farpel smiling somewhat oddly, although it was a bit challenging to determine 'somewhat oddly' where it concerned the smile of a Kinglorf, but somehow, she managed to reach that conclusion. "Mr. Farpel, may I ask why you're smiling in that manner?"

Farpel continued smiling. "Well, lady, it's just that you're still worried about those creatures outside listening in to your conversations. I kinda took care of that when I was here the last time."

On hearing this, Mrs. Hensworthy had mixed feelings; if, in fact, Farpel had neutralized the listening capabilities of those spies parked on the lane, she would be quite relieved. What concerned her was the *manner* in which he might have accomplished that task. She was hoping the agents hadn't been somehow vaporized; that would be *quite* awkward to explain to the authorities. "May I ask what, exactly, you did to 'take care of that?'" For emphasis, Mrs. Hensworthy added quotes to Farpel's expression.

"Oh, nothing too serious, lady. I just used dimensional folding and a couple of micro-rifts in certain 3-spaces, and joined the receptive part of their listening device to an especially noisy all-night restaurant I know on Measel. And I'm sure you guys know from your experience with our buddy Brobding Measelfort, without a GadgiYack, all you can get from a Measeloot is a bunch of squeaks, clicks and weird tones. Trying to figure that out ought to keep those guys occupied for a while."

Both Malthorp and Mrs. Hensworthy now wore broad smiles of their own. It was then that Malthorp remembered the question posed by Mrs. Hensworthy earlier. "Tell us, Mr. Farpel, however did you manage to get that commercial on television? And, in particular, why did you choose The Potted Plant Channel as the venue for airing it?"

Farpel was a bit confused. "The Potted Plant Channel? No, no, I don't think you get the picture. That commercial aired on *every* digital feed emanating from what you guys refer to as 'cable companies' and 'streaming services.' *Everywhere.* As in everywhere on this puny planet. Oh, sorry about the 'puny;' I'm just accustomed to dealing with bigger rocks. My Kinglorf buddies and I used a GadgiYack interface to generate the voiceover in every language we needed, wherever the commercial aired. Then we hacked the digital feeds, and introduced our little video in place of whatever commercial was supposed to air at the very next time point. It was pretty basic stuff for us. Yeah, planetary Biepal sales levels should go through the upper atmosphere, so to speak."

Malthorp and Mrs. Hensworthy were impressed, but Mrs. Hensworthy had a thought. "Oh, dear, you don't suppose that annoying Colonel Messington saw the commercial, do you? He's bound to wonder how that video was acquired."

And just as she finished her sentence, there was a substantial banging on the front door of their cottage. They all looked rather surprised; Farpel took the banging as a cue, and rose toward the ceiling.

"I think I can leave this matter to you, Hensworthys. I'll be in touch!" And with that, he disappeared through the rift in the ceiling, and the rift quickly disappeared. Mrs. Hensworthy headed for the door, as the banging became more emphatic.

She opened the door to see Colonel Messington, followed by Sergeant Major DeLade Greene, and what appeared to be two underlings. She decided to play it cool, so to speak, and make herself quite the congenial hostess. "Why

Colonel Messington, what a pleasant surprise! And Sergeant Major Greene, always lovely to see you. How may I help you?"

The Sergeant Major pushed his way forward, and spoke rather loudly. "Right, then, madam, we are here to confiscate all of your electronics! All of them! And we have a number of questions to which we will want answers! A number, I say!"

Colonel Messington stepped in behind him. "Please do be quiet, Sergeant Major! I'll speak with the lady, if you do not mind!"

The Sergeant Major stepped aside. "Right, sir, sorry, sir; just trying to help!"

"You can help best, Sergeant Major, by waiting outside!" And with that, Colonel Messington directed Sergeant Major Greene back out the door, and closed it behind him.

"May I join you briefly, Mrs. Hensworthy?" The Colonel proceeded into the living room, mumbling as he went, "Perhaps it's time to send that fool Greene back to the Arctic, or wherever it is they kept him occupied earlier."

"May I offer you a cup of tea, Colonel?" Mrs. Hensworthy continued the 'cool' act as the Colonel sat down.

"Why, yes, thank you, Mrs. Hensworthy. I must say, I expected rather a different reception. And excuse me, but I don't believe I've met this gentleman," referring to Malthorp.

Mrs. Hensworthy let the 'different reception' comment slide unanswered. "Oh yes, where are my manners? This is my husband Malthorp. Malthorp, Colonel Messington, of whom we've spoken recently."

Malthorp put on his friendliest face. "Charmed, I'm sure, Colonel."

"I'll be back in a moment with some refreshment. Why don't you two get acquainted?" And with that, Mrs. Hensworthy made a hasty exit toward the kitchen, praying the whole time that Brobding Measelfort wouldn't choose this moment to drop in through a rift in the middle of the bookcase. Aside from being utterly catastrophic with respect to placating the Colonel, it would make for some rather awkward explanations.

Mrs. Hensworthy returned with a tray forthwith. "And what have you two men of the world been discussing in my absence?"

"Well, my dear, I was just explaining to the Colonel my experiences with respect to the sociological expeditions I pursued in my younger days at various points around the globe." A barely noticeable wink from Malthorp reassured Mrs. Hensworthy that he had diplomatically managed the conversation.

They were all seated, tea in hand, when Mrs. Hensworthy opened the conversation. "Now, Colonel, to what do we owe the honor of your visit today to our humble cottage?"

The Colonel smiled. "Now, now, Mrs. Hensworthy, you and I both know why I've made an appearance here, today in particular. And I would prefer not to call that idiot Greene back in here to proceed with a search for digital files. So why don't you tell me just how it is that the video I showed you in my office several days ago has ended up on the telly as a COMMERCIAL ADVERTISEMENT FOR *BIEPAL*?!" The Colonel raised his voice rather substantially as he completed the question.

Mrs. Hensworthy did her best to look surprised. "Why, Colonel Messington, whatever do you mean? I have no awareness of any commercials on the telly containing that video. Malthorp, my dear, have you seen anything on the telly related to that video I described to you after visiting the good Colonel?"

The Colonel sat there looking particularly frustrated as Malthorp immediately chimed in. "Why, no, my dear, I certainly haven't seen anything of that ilk. And from the description you provided..."

At that point, Colonel Messington decided it was time to interrupt. "All right, ALL RIGHT, I get the picture! You're going to play ignorant with me. All right, then, you don't leave me with many alternatives. I'll need to review your electronics forthwith." The Colonel headed toward the front door to re-admit Sergeant Major Greene and the two underlings to the room.

Mrs. Hensworthy flashed a concerned look toward Malthorp; he was doing his best to remain calm. He reached for the laptop on the side table near Mrs. Hensworthy.

The Colonel observed Malthorp moving the laptop as he returned to the living room with the Sergeant Major's team. "I'll just take that, thank you very much. Also, your phones, if you please." The men stood there awaiting the electronics in question.

"Why, of course, Colonel, here is the laptop." Malthorp handed over the laptop, and his favorite tablet. "I don't happen to have a mobile phone, but here is a tablet I use often to read the news. My dear, perhaps you'd be good enough to give your phone to the good Colonel." Mrs. Hensworthy passed her phone to Colonel Messington rather hesitantly.

"Thank you for your notable cooperation." Colonel Messington was apparently in a sarcastic mood. "And without going into a long diatribe asking me what exactly I mean by 'electronic devices,' or some such nonsense as that, do you have any other data-related gadgets in which we might have an interest?" The Hensworthys both nodded indicating a negative response to the Colonel's inquiry. "We will review these immediately, and return them to you." With that, the Colonel and his cohort headed out the door.

As the door closed, Mrs. Hensworthy looked frantic. "But, Malthorp, the video! It's on the laptop! He's going to know we stole it somehow! Oh, dear, how will we explain the presence of that video on the laptop?"

"Relax, my dear. The video is no longer on the drive."

Mrs. Hensworthy looked askance at Malthorp. "What do you mean, 'no longer on the drive?' How is that possible?"

Malthorp wore a rather smug expression. "Well, I haven't needed to use it much since I arrived here, but Jordalakians can generate a small external electrical charge when necessary. I used it a couple of times when I needed a flashlight and the batteries happened to be drained."

"You'll recall that I made a point of picking up the laptop, and handing it over to our friend Colonel Messington? Well, as I picked it up, I introduced an electrical charge to the unit, and sort of fried the hard drive. They won't be seeing a video on that computer any time soon."

"Why, Malthorp, that's wonderful! Wait a minute, that's also terrible! I had a lot of recipes, book lists and plant care instructions on that laptop! What am I supposed to do now?!"

Malthorp smiled. "If you recall, my dear, Mr. Farpel's Padgenok Dragon absorbed all the data from that laptop, and he said it was merely a matter of a squeeze behind the wings to recover it. I'm sure if we contact him promptly, Mr. Farpel can bring the little beast back, and restore all of your data to another platform."

"Malthorp, my dear, have I mentioned lately that you're absolutely brilliant?"

"I appreciate the compliment, my dear; shall we make another pot of tea?"

14

"Nothing?   What do you mean, nothing?!" Colonel Messington was standing inside a large, specialized van parked outside the Hensworthy residence. The van was filled with electronic wizardry designed to extricate files from hard drives. He was addressing the two underlings, who were supposedly whiz bang at, as the Colonel expressed it, 'all these electronic and computer thingamabobs.'   "How can there be nothing?"

Whiz Kid 1 looked back blankly at the Colonel. "There's nothing, sir; the laptop appears to be completely devoid of information. It looks to me like the drive was subjected to some kind of electrical charge or something; the memory chips and hard drive are nonfunctional."

The Colonel wore a notably annoyed expression. "If it's a piece of trash, then why did they even *give* it to us?" Turning his head toward Whiz Kid 2, he continued with his inquiry. "And what do the tablet and mobile phone have to tell us, Corporal?"

Whiz Kid 2 looked rather forlorn. "Well, sir, I think... that is... I mean to say..."

The Colonel's patience was being tested. "Just spit it out, man!"

"Well, sir, from what I've found so far, the tablet has essentially nothing but some news links."

The Colonel waited. When nothing else was forthcoming, he felt it necessary to speak up. "And the phone?! What about the phone, Corporal?!"

Oh, yes, the phone; well, sir, on the phone, I found some contacts, a collection of recipes, and several 'how-to' files related to potted plant care."

The Colonel just looked at him for a long moment. "Recipes."

"Yes, sir."

"And potted plants."

"Yes, sir, that's all I'm finding here. On the bright side, there does seem to be a really nice recipe for sponge cake."

The added 'sponge cake' remark didn't help matters. "*I* don't care about *sponge cake*, Corporal! we're talking about a global economic upheaval, and you're offering me a *sponge cake recipe*!"

The Colonel did his best to remain calm. "Well, at least it's something to look at. Copy all the data, Corporal; perhaps the recipes or potted plant files are in some sort of code and contain something more interesting. And make sure you get all the contacts. We'll go through those with a fine-toothed comb; perhaps there's someone there who would be useful in tying the Hensworthys to this Biepal business."

"While you're doing that, the Sergeant Major and I are going back to the cottage. That useless laptop may be a decoy to deflect us from finding the real one. Well, we shall just see about *that*!"

With that, the Colonel and Sergeant Major Greene returned to the front door of the cottage; the Sergeant Major knocked rather vigorously.

A moment later, Mrs. Hensworthy opened the door. "Why, gentlemen, back so soon?"

The men moved into the foyer, and the Colonel responded forthwith. "Don't play coy with us, Mrs. Hensworthy. You must have known that laptop was useless. So be so kind as to tell us, madam, where is the real computer? We'd prefer to avoid a potentially messy search of the premises."

Mrs. Hensworthy offered as pleasant a look as she could manage. "I can assure you, Colonel, we have no other electronics that would be of interest to you. However, you're welcome to peruse the premises. We do have a small telly in the kitchen, but I doubt you'll find that very exciting. Oh, and if you go into the solarium, do be careful of Penelope."

The Colonel raised his eyebrows. "Penelope? Do you have someone else residing on the premises, Mrs. Hensworthy?"

"Why no, Colonel, Penelope happens to be my new favorite philodendron plant."

The Colonel just stood there. "Your philodendron plant."

"That's correct, and she's very sensitive to strangers, so I'll thank you to move slowly and speak very quietly if you happen to be in her vicinity."

"A sensitive philodendron plant. Uh huh." The Colonel's eyes just sort of glazed over at that point. He and the Sergeant Major then began rummaging around the premises.

Approximately 7.362 minutes later, they reconvened in the foyer. "Well, Sergeant Major?"

"Nothing to report with respect to electronics, sir. I did find a highly suspect collection of snow globes, however! Highly suspect, I say! I believe that would certainly be worth our further investigation."

"Snow globes, you say?"

"Yes, sir; I must say, several of them appeared to have very little snow indeed. Perhaps they're hiding something *sinister*!" He looked pointedly at the Hensworthys.

The Colonel shook his head. "Or perhaps they're just shoddy snow globes, Sergeant Major."

He turned to Mrs. Hensworthy. "Well, madam, this round to you, I believe. You haven't heard the last of this, however. We'll be watching!" The Colonel made his way to the door, with the Sergeant Major following closely behind, still babbling something about suspect snow globes. The door closed behind them.

Mrs. Hensworthy pushed aside a curtain, and peeked out the window to ensure they had gone. "I thought they'd never leave! I was rather worried that they might try to inspect the shed and find your vessel, Malthorp."

Malthorp didn't look particularly concerned. "Oh, that. It's quite well sealed against intrusion, my dear. If someone happens upon it, I'm sure they would be satisfied if you tell them that you're a big science fiction fan, and it's a related lawn ornament you picked up at one of those space fantasy conventions."

The next day, the Hensworthys were discussing the purchase of a new laptop to replace the one Malthorp had to destroy in order to keep Colonel Messington from discovering the video they had 'borrowed' from his office. Mrs. Hensworthy had a thought.

"You know, I was in Harrogate the other day, and there appears to be a very pleasant establishment just down the street from one of the tea shops. It had all sorts of electronics, mobile phones, televisions and other such doodads in the window. I thought perhaps we might make an excursion of it, and buy a nice laptop from there. I do prefer to frequent the local shops when we can, rather than those huge, impersonal online conglomerates."

Malthorp nodded. "I quite agree, my dear. We can have lunch in town, and make an afternoon of it." Malthorp paused as he drew aside a curtain and peeked out the front window. "And if we do it just right, I believe we can give Colonel Messington's spies some well-needed exercise in the process. They do seem to spend an inordinate amount of time just lolling about in that spy truck of theirs, peering through their vacuum cleaner, or whatever that spyglass of theirs is called."

Mrs. Hensworthy had a gleam in her eye as she thought about the possibilities. "Oh, I do like the sound of that."

After a brief strategy discussion, they made ready, and headed for the door. Once outside, they ran toward their car parked in the driveway toward the back of the cottage, an immaculately kept 2006 Jaguar S-class with a beautiful pale-blue metallic paint finish. They then: opened all the doors and the boot; ran to their shed; threw some bags from the shed into the back seat and boot; closed up the back doors and boot; climbed into the vehicle; hurriedly closed the front doors; and drove off fairly dramatically in a direction opposite that of Harrogate. The bags actually contained some clothing they had assembled for the upcoming semi-annual charitable clothing drive; they also threw in a bag of leaves they had gathered from the back lawn earlier that week. But of course, Colonel Messington's people didn't know that.

Observing them from the vacuum cleaner repair truck, Cora Nosely and Malcolm Schlectwetter were sure that the Hensworthys were trying to make a hasty exit with some sort of contraband. "Hurry up, Malcolm, they're going to get away! We need to follow them! Like, now!"

In a moment, Malcolm was behind the wheel of the truck, following closely behind the Hensworthy's Jaguar after making an awkward multi-point turn-around in the narrow lane. "I'm following them, Cora, but then what?"

"Malcolm, do try to keep up! We need to see where they're taking the stuff. And don't follow them so closely! We don't want them to *know* that we know about the illicit goods, for goodness sakes!"

Malcolm did his best to drive at a discreet distance behind the Hensworthy get-away car. It is, in fact, rather challenging to be discreet when one is driving a large and somewhat dilapidated truck clearly marked 'Vacuum Cleaner Repair' in enormous letters. 'Blending in' is not what you would call its strong suit.

Malthorp made a point of driving rather quickly, as if he was trying to evade his pursuers. About ten minutes into the drive, he swerved rather suddenly, and then returned to the center of their lane.

Mrs. Hensworthy was intrigued. "Tell me, Malthorp, was that some sort of evasive maneuver to better elude our spies?"

Malthorp glanced in her direction. "Why, no, my dear; didn't you see that poor fuzzy caterpillar on the road? And it was making quite a noticeable sound as it ambulated along. It was a markedly decorative specimen, and I thought it prudent to allow the poor creature to reach the other side of the road, rather than meet with our tires, which would have been quite the unpleasant experience for all parties concerned."

"You swerved around a caterpillar? However did you manage to see it, and even more amazingly, *hear* it, and so quickly?"

Malthorp smiled. "Please recall, Eleanora, that as a Jordalakian, my vision and hearing are rather more acute than those of the indigenous species. The caterpillar was really quite obvious to me. Really, my dear, I don't know how your species manages with the limited faculties you have on board, so to speak." Mrs. Hensworthy just nodded her head in disbelief.

As mentioned earlier, the Hensworthys were proceeding in the wrong direction intentionally, so as to give poor Cora and Malcolm a pleasantly circuitous journey through the countryside before arriving in Harrogate. Malthorp planned to take them about an hour out of the way. Just to make things a bit more interesting, about 30 minutes enroute, they stopped the car to drop off one of the bags at a municipal recycling center.

The truck drove past the point where Malthorp had turned off, and Malcolm parked the vehicle on the side of the road. Cora then watched as Mrs. Hensworthy hurriedly took a bag out of the car and deposited it in a receptacle. "Hah! Alright, Malcolm, we have them now! They just dumped some of the contraband in a bin on that property. Let's wait until they pull out, and we'll drive in and retrieve the goods!"

Mrs. Hensworthy got back in the car, and Malthorp proceeded to drive past the spy truck and continue on their journey.

"Cora, if we stop now, they're going to get away."

"Listen, Malcolm, it's important we get that bag! We'll just have to try and catch up. Now pull in so I can grab the bag from the bin."

Malcolm continued to mumble something to the effect of "Ok, I'm telling you, we're going to lose them... we're losing them... yep, it looks like we've lost them, but you have to have the bag, so we'll get the bag. We're getting the bag." Or something along that general theme, as he backed up the truck and pulled into the municipal facility.

Cora leapt out of the truck, grabbed the bag from the bin, and jumped back in. "Ok, I've got it; let's go!" And with that, Malcolm took off in the same direction taken moments earlier by the Hensworthys.

As he drove, Cora attired herself in some clothing suitable for handling hazardous materials, and took a respirator out of a box, in case there was any sort of poisonous gas to contend with in the bag. Malcolm observed her as he looked over his shoulder. "Uh, Cora, what are you doing?"

Cora grimaced at him. "What do you mean, 'what am I doing?' Who knows what kind of alien stuff they might have in here! If I'm going to open this thing, I'm not taking any chances."

"Uh, Cora, in case you haven't noticed, I happen to be in this same vehicle. You know, same air, etc.. If you're really that worried, don't you think that perhaps I should put on some gear before you open that bag?"

"Oh, don't be such a wimp, Malcolm! Just keep driving. I'm going to see what we're dealing with here." And with that, she donned her respirator, and carefully opened the bag. There were leaves.

Malcolm kept his eyes on the road, although he was now quite concerned about the contents of the bag, and he still didn't see the Hensworthy car anywhere in front of him. "Well, Cora, what's in the bag?"

Cora did some rummaging around in the bag. There were just more leaves.

"Uh, Cora? Anything to worry about back there? Anything hazardous?"

Cora tore off her respirator, looking sad and feeling rather disappointed. "Malcolm, just shut up and drive, will you?"

15

The Hensworthys had a lovely lunch at a small café in Harrogate, and proceeded to buy a new laptop at the local electronics shop. They remained in the village for quite a while, to give the vacuum cleaner repair truck time to catch up, but it never appeared, so after a delightful stroll through town, they returned home.

They had been settled in the living room for perhaps an hour when they heard the distinctive rattling, coughing sound of a dilapidated truck rolling up the lane. As Mrs. Hensworthy peeked out the window, the vacuum cleaner repair truck once again parked across the lane from their cottage.

"Well, Malthorp, they seem to be back. I wonder where they wandered off to after we lost them at the Recycling Center? I do hope they enjoyed the leaves we left for them."

Malthorp smiled. "Well, at least we gave them a bit of an outing. After all, it must get quite tiring sitting in the same spot day after day. And I thought the leaves were certainly a nice touch. Something of a little mystery to stimulate their brain cells."

Mrs. Hensworthy picked up the new laptop they had acquired. "Oh, I do hope that nice Mr. Farpel makes an appearance soon with his little pet dragon; I would love to get my recipes restored to this gadget already."

"Patience, my dear; Mr. Farpel is due to receive another box of carrots tomorrow, I believe, in payment for his Biepal deliveries; we'll simply leave him a holo-message."

That evening, Malthorp placed another recorded message in the box of carrots left in the foyer for Farpel, and, as expected, an interdimensional rift opened in the Hensworthy living room ceiling the following afternoon as Farpel dropped in for a visit.

"Greetings, Barnorklets. Message received, as they say."

At that point, Farpel was, of course, completely unintelligible to the Hensworthys, who heard only a series of odd grunts and somewhat curious melodic tones as Farpel tried to communicate. Mrs. Hensworthy withdrew her GadgiYack from the side table, and handed another to Malthorp. "Sorry, Mr. Farpel, I didn't have my GadgiYack in place. Again, please?"

Farpel seemed just a bit exasperated. "I was *saying* 'Greetings, Barnorklets.' *In any case*, you mentioned in your message that you needed the data from my Padgenok Dragon, and I was curious as to why. I didn't delete the data from your thingamabob earlier; just copied it."

Malthorp chimed in. "Well, unfortunately, Mr. Farpel, I had to fry the storage media on that device in order to keep the ever-annoying Colonel Messington from discovering the video we acquired from his office."

Farpel displayed an expression one might interpret as 'distaste.' "Fried storage media doesn't sound very palatable. Now, of course, if you happened to be having lunch with some residents of Margon 12, those beasties really enjoying crunching on electronics for some reason. I guess it takes all kinds. So I assume you have a new gadget that you'd like my

Dragon to squat on? Lucky for you, the Dragon didn't expunge the data yet. Padgenok Dragons can hold onto quite a bit of electromagnetic content."

Mrs. Hensworthy handed the laptop to Farpel, who promptly opened it, and placed his Dragon once again on the keyboard. As before, it looked like a big purple worm at first, and then suddenly sprouted four beautiful wings and an arrow-pointed tail. Farpel gave it a squeeze behind the wings, and the dragon changed to a somewhat lighter shape of purple, bordering on pink.

"Yeah, it's doing its thing. I may need to review the data afterward; this little guy hasn't expunged in a while, so there may be some, shall we say, 'extraneous' data from other sources that's going to show up on this thing."

Approximately 3.784 minutes later, the Dragon returned to purple worm form. "Ok, we're good. Let me just look at the data, and delete anything you might find to be totally weird." Farpel put the Dragon back in its satchel, and just stared at the keyboard. "Yeah, I'm kinda not used to anything this primitive. Can you show me something that tells me what data is on board, lady?"

Mrs. Hensworthy took the device, brought up a file directory, and handed it back to Farpel. He perused the listings. Luckily, the laptop had a touch screen, and Farpel was able to highlight all the files that needed to be deleted. "Yeah, lose these files, if you'd be so kind. I don't think you want to know what's in those data sets."

Mrs. Hensworthy proceeded to delete the range of files that Farpel had highlighted. Malthorp had a thought. "My dear, would you also be good enough to delete that Kinglorf video from the laptop as well? We don't need the good Colonel Messington coming back to discover it on this device."

"Good idea, Malthorp." She perused the list of files, found the video, and deleted it from the drive. She then expunged all the files from the 'deleted files' location. She turned to Farpel. "Mr. Farpel, I'm curious, how did you know which files belonged to us? I don't recall that you can read our writing."

"Oh, that's easy, lady. I know the character sets used to name any data that the Dragon had munched on earlier; I just looked for all the files that used a character set I didn't recognize, and figured those were yours."

"Mr. Farpel, you are a clever fellow."

"I appreciate the thought, lady. Well, Barnorklets, I have places to be, and creatures to see. If there's nothing else, I'll be on my way." With that, Farpel rose to the ceiling and passed through the interdimensional rift as it closed behind him.

Mrs. Hensworthy watched as the ceiling returned to its rather humdrum form. "He is a helpful fellow, isn't he?" Malthorp nodded in agreement.

Meanwhile, strange things were happening in various other locales on this fairly blue-colored orb that humans call home.

The Taller vs. Shorter controversy continued on multiple fronts. Since home builders are notorious for taking a 'cookie cutter' approach to building, where every house looks like every other house in order to save money, entire housing developments were now being devoted exclusively to Tallers or Shorters.

New clothing and sporting goods stores were popping up in the malls and online, catering specifically to the Taller clientele.

Last but not least, certain auto manufacturers had begun offering absolutely enormous Sport Utility Vehicles, which they now labeled Tremendous Utility Buggies, or 'TUBs.' These vehicles provided extraordinary headroom and legroom in each row of seating, so that the nine foot tall driver felt quite comfortable accessing the steering wheel and pedals. The response from environmentalists bordered on the insane, since at least one of these vehicles actually needed to use the measure *Gallons per Mile* to reflect its fuel usage, but Tallers absolutely loved the roomy interiors. A small group of Shorters were also seen to be buying these behemoths, primarily for conversion into motor homes or weekend retreats.

As for Colonel Messington, he felt utterly frustrated in his efforts to determine the source of Biepal. After examining Mrs. Hensworthy's phone, the Colonel's staff noticed a beverage distributor in the contacts list, and Colonel Messington had his team pursue an investigation on that front.

Unfortunately, they determined that the beverage distributor shown in the contacts was a smallish London subsidiary of a company located in Kenmare, Ireland that was, in turn, a division of a corporate entity in Curaçao, which was a wholly owned satellite of a conglomerate registered on the Isle of Man, with a mailing address in Bermuda, that apparently had all its mail forwarded to one of the smaller mailboxes at a United Parcel Service store located in the United States in Weehawken, New Jersey, that at that moment was assigned to Wally's Wallaby Warehouse, a pet store situated in Adelaide, Australia that, in point of fact, had absolutely nothing to do with wallabies, but did carry a variety of fish, hermit crabs and assorted small furry creatures. While Wally, the proprietor of the pet store, was happy to discuss some very attractive guinea pigs the store had available that week, and claimed they made excellent pets, he in fact knew absolutely, positively nothing about Biepal.

16

While various companies, suppliers, retailers and manufacturers were managing to adjust nicely to the new demand presented by the dichotomy of Tallers and Shorters in the population, governments continued to panic. Panic was, after all, part of their job. The various authorities were absolutely stumped as to what to do in order to get a handle on, as they so often referred to it, "this Biepal business."

"Mr. President, we've taken our investigations about as far they can go. We've gone so far as to work cooperatively with our counterparts in Europe and at NATO Headquarters, which I'm sure you realize is quite out of character when it comes to top secret issues such as this. Still, nothing concrete." General Dithering, the director of the top-secret operation known as TEXTING, was once again in the Oval Office, briefing President Hemminhough on the latest Biepal findings, or perhaps we should say 'lack thereof.'

"One of our domestic intelligence units believes this Biepal substance may be part of a subversive plot by a group of radicals calling themselves the Patriots for a Taller America, originating somewhere in the Pacific Northwest, but we haven't been able to verify that, sir."

The President wore a look of studied concern, or at least the expression he was told to assume by his press people when he wanted to convey the impression of 'studied concern.' "Well, Dithering, by gum, we need to do *something* about this! We don't want contributors to assume we're just ignoring it! And by contributors, of course, I mean the population, the population, man! And for goodness sakes, don't go quoting me on that. Haven't those blasted drug companies come up with anything of interest?"

Dithering searched through his briefcase, and referred briefly to some notes he had brought along in a folder. "Well, Mr. President, from the latest reports, Extrilax Pharmaceuticals is continuing in its clinical trials of two possible medications, to see if they can provide any benefit with long-term application, but the results haven't been particularly promising. One group is extraordinarily short, and another seems to have a problem with, if I'm reading this correctly, purple fur."

For lack of a better alternative, the President remained with his 'studied concern' look. "Look, Dithering, we have so many regulations in this great nation of ours, can't we get *some* regulatory body to get this Biepal stuff under control?! I mean, honestly, it's getting so that some of our Congress people need to stand in the middle of the Capitol rotunda so they don't hit their heads on the lower portions of the ceiling!"

The gentlemen contemplated the issue for some moments, and Dithering had a thought. "Well, Mr. President, we might consider placing Biepal under the auspices of the Food and Drug Administration; you know, regulated substance, war on drugs, and all that sort."

"Dithering, that *is* an interesting thought. Let me dwell on that for a bit... Ok, I've dwelled on it long enough. Get in touch with the Director, Chief or whatever the big cheese is called over at the FDA, and see if we can't get them to wrap some controls around this Biepal business."

General Dithering subsequently worked his way through channels to arrange a meeting with Marjorie Tapparatchnik, the Commissioner of the FDA. Three days after seeing the President, he was in her office for a meeting.

"Commissioner, we have a serious issue here, and we're convinced that the FDA offers the right mechanism to get this under control."

Dr. Tapparatchnik nodded her head in agreement. "We've actually been monitoring these Biepal effects for several months now, General. I tend to agree with you that this is an unusual situation, and we need to step in to protect the public once again."

"It's taken us somewhat longer than expected to evaluate the substance. Lab people supposedly keep ingesting it 'accidentally,' and suddenly become quite disinterested in evaluating it further. As a result, we keep running out of lab people. But I think we finally have a handle on it now, and the FDA is prepared to issue a ruling that limits access to Biepal only by prescription from a qualified physician." She lowered her voice markedly, continuing in practically a whisper. "The next question, of course, is what physician is actually qualified to write such a prescription, but I'm sure we can find one or two practitioners, so that people don't accuse us of actually banning the substance outright. Wink, wink."

The General just looked at her; he wasn't sure what to make of 'wink, wink,' but the important thing was, the FDA was going to get this Biepal stuff locked up. "All right, Dr. Tapparatchnik, I'll leave it to you to get this done. Let's try to make this as expedient as possible, shall we?"

Within 30 days (based on the usual Earthly rotations), the FDA came out with guidance indicating that Biepal was to be available only to select laboratories for medical and scientific evaluation. As for the public, it would be available only as a highly controlled substance, by medical prescription.

Even for those beings separated dimensionally from the Earth, they could practically hear the uproar from the public on receiving this announcement. The retailers that offered

Biepal, as well as the Tallers who enjoyed consuming it, were absolutely incensed that the government was now going to limit their access to the beverage. Even some of the more argumentative Shorters were protesting this interference, but that was primarily because they just enjoyed complaining and yelling at someone.

Word traveled quickly from the local distributors back to the original distributor in London, and subsequently, to the Hensworthys. Mrs. Hensworthy received a call approximately 2.144 days after the FDA announcement.

"Malthorp, we may have a little problem on our hands."

As Mrs. Hensworthy addressed him, Malthorp was busy perusing the news on his tablet. "Yes, my dear, I think I'm aware of the subject at hand. I just read an article indicating that the Americans are planning to restrict Biepal to medicinal uses, or some such rubbish as that. According to what I just saw, some of the European governments may follow suit. I think it's time we left another message for Mr. Farpel."

Two days later, Dearlotin Farpelmop was retrieving his most recent box of carrots in payment for Biepal deliveries, and saw the holo-recorder in the box. "Now what?" he thought to himself as he activated the device.

When the Hensworthys awoke the next morning, and came downstairs to enjoy their breakfast, Farpel was waiting for them in the living room. Mrs. Hensworthy was the first to notice him. She immediately donned a GadgiYack.

"Why Mr. Farpel, here so early?"

"I came for my carrots, saw your message, and decided to stick around for the fun. Are these creatures joking? They want to control Biepal as if it's some sort of dangerous substance?"

Malthorp chimed in. "Well, Mr. Farpel, it *is* making people taller, after all, although I do believe the authorities have taken this a bit far."

"Taller, schmaller! Who cares if some of you creatures get a little taller! You're too short anyway. And this is going to put a serious crimp in our sales." Farpel developed a sudden, rather obvious gleam in his eyes. "I think I'll need to do something about this."

As was usually the case when Farpel suggested he was going to take some kind of action, Mrs. Hensworthy wasn't sure she liked the sound of it. "Now, Mr. Farpel, you're not going to do anything extreme, like vaporize some people or anything like that, are you? We can't have people disappearing into nothingness over a beverage! And we certainly don't want anyone to know about that little matter of Biepal's rather extraterrestrial origins!"

"Lady, why do you think I'm going to vaporize somebody? You know, if I didn't know better, I'd say you have some kind of weird prejudice against otherworldly beings, the way you always jump to the conclusion that we're going to do something terrible."

Mrs. Hensworthy adopted an apologetic tone. "Oh, I am sorry, Mr. Farpel, I'm just not sure what we can do about this. So, what exactly *are* you going to do?"

"Leave that to me, lady; having observed this species and its obsessions for a while, I have a few ideas. Let's just say I'm going to get their attention, and they might just find that they need to change their minds about this control stuff."

Several days later, the Hensworthys had no further word from Farpel. In order to take their minds off the current issue with Biepal, they decided to make an evening of it in town, and enjoy dinner at The Mouse and Elephant, one of the more delightful local eateries. Of course, they were accompanied by their favorite spies, Cora Nosely and Malcolm Schlectwetter, who were their constant companions of late, in a manner of speaking. Malthorp drove slowly enough to ensure that Cora and Malcolm didn't get lost this time. Mrs. Hensworthy kept an eye on the vacuum cleaner repair truck through the back window. "It's so nice that we can give the young people a little outing now and then, isn't it, Malthorp?"

Malthorp nodded. "Yes, my dear, but I do wonder how long we're going to have them in our midst." He thought about it for a moment. "Although they don't really require much care. I suppose they're very much like those succulent plants in many ways; the occasional watering and they're perfectly happy."

"Oh, Malthorp, I really don't think our spies would appreciate it if we watered them. Especially with all that nice electronic equipment in their truck. I do see the analogy, however."

They arrived at The Mouse and Elephant, and parked nearby. The vacuum cleaner repair truck parked similarly, about half a block away. As the Hensworthys proceeded into the restaurant, Malthorp took notice as the vacuum cleaner on display on top of the truck turned in their direction. "Well, their periscope gadget just adjusted to our current course. It's nice to know they're keeping an eye on us. It does make one feel so secure."

The maître d' directed the Hensworthys to a very nice table near the window, and they ensconced themselves and ordered a bottle of wine. "Now, Malthorp, do be careful! You know how you react to alcoholic beverages."

"Yes, yes, my dear, just a sip for now. As I'm driving, feel free to indulge, and we can take the remainder of the bottle home."

Some moments later, as they were enjoying a lovely seafood dinner, a murmuring arose around the restaurant. It slowly grew in volume as customers stared at their mobile phones, and several patrons suddenly had a rather panicked look upon their faces. The volume continued to increase.

A woman at the next table leaned over toward Mrs. Hensworthy, and asked in a seemingly fearful tone, "Excuse me for asking, but do you have any mobile phone reception?"

Mrs. Hensworthy made it a point to leave her phone in her purse when dining or otherwise engaging in entertainments, so she had no awareness as to the reception, or lack thereof, on her device. In order to respond to the inquiry, she took her phone out briefly. "Just a moment, dear, my phone is tucked away... here it is. Why, no, I don't seem to have any signal. Is there a problem?"

The woman wore a worried expression as she thanked Mrs. Hensworthy for checking, and returned to the conversation with her dining companion, now fraught with concern.

The murmuring continued as most patrons returned to their meals. Several ran out the door looking somewhat frantic. One man was heard to exclaim rather loudly, "OMG! My texts! What will I do without my texts?!" Yes, he actually said the letters 'O' 'M' 'G.' Those silly humans.

Exactly one hour later, every mobile phone in the establishment, for lack of a better term, 'dinged.' Malthorp and Mrs. Hensworthy just looked at each other, and Malthorp thought the event worthy of comment. "Well, that *was* a curiosity! Eleanora, my dear, if you'd be so kind, take a quick gander at your phone, and see if there's some sort of message."

Mrs. Hensworthy took out her phone once again, and looked at the screen. Much to Malthorp's surprise, given the panic that now seemed to be enveloping the restaurant, Mrs. Hensworthy smiled, but quickly replaced her smile with a frown, in keeping with the tone of the room. She handed her phone to Malthorp, who looked at the screen in turn. Here is what he saw:

BIEPAL IS YOURS TO ENJOY. DO NOT ATTEMPT TO STOP OR REGULATE THE SUPPLY. IF YOU COMPLY, ALL WILL BE WELL. IF YOU DO NOT COMPLY, YOU WILL HENCEFORTH BE PHONELESS. FOREVER.

THE CHOICE IS YOURS.

Upon seeing the message, Malthorp couldn't help but smile as well. A quick gesture from Mrs. Hensworthy, however, and Malthorp immediately adopted a much more serious expression. He made a point of speaking in lowered tones. "Well, Eleanora, he's done it again! I must say, he *is* quite good at playing these games!"

Mrs. Hensworthy nodded. "How in the world did he do it, I wonder? We really must ask him, the next time he drops in for his carrots."

The Hensworthys finished up a delightful piece of flourless chocolate cake they were sharing, and paid the restaurant fare. The waiter then brought over a paper bag, containing a little something special that the Hensworthys had ordered, and they prepared to depart.

As they returned to the street outside the restaurant, Malthorp moved in the direction of the car. Mrs. Hensworthy, however, had a task to complete. "Malthorp, dear, why don't you bring the car around? I'll only be a moment."

"Of course, my dear; see you shortly." With that, Mrs. Hensworthy walked in the direction of the vacuum cleaner repair truck. Cora Nosely made note of Mrs. Hensworthy's progress, observing her through the vacuum cleaner periscope. "Malcolm, she's headed this way! Right for the truck!"

"Huh; I wonder why she would do that."

"Is that all you have to say, Malcolm? Should we do something?"

Before they could take any action, Mrs. Hensworthy knocked on the back door of the vehicle. Cora had a somewhat frantic look. "*Now* what?! What should I do?"

"Uh, try answering the door."

Cora opened the door cautiously, to find Mrs. Hensworthy standing there, handing her a bag.

"Good evening, dear; we thought you might like something to eat while you're doing your observing and whatnot. Enjoy!" And with that, Mrs. Hensworthy turned around, and took two steps to their Jaguar, which Malthorp had driven to her current locale. She entered the vehicle, and they proceeded down the road toward home.

Cora closed the door, and turned. She and Malcolm just looked at each other.

"Cora, I think they might be on to us."

"You *think*?! Quick, Malcolm, hand me that respirator. Who knows what kind of devious stuff they could have placed in this bag!"

"Well, she said it was food, but all right, here's the mask." Malcolm reached back and handed the rather ominous-looking respirator mask to Cora.

After she had carefully donned the mask, she prepared to open the bag. "Malcolm, don't you want to put on a mask?"

"You know, Cora, based on our recent experience with the leaves, I think I'll take my chances."

Cora gave him an annoyed look, and very slowly, very carefully opened the bag. Inside, she found two take-out dinners consisting of, on the one hand, fillet of sole, and on the other hand, roast chicken. There were also some vegetables, and a nice baked potato. And a small box of cookies.

"Well, Cora?"

Cora handed the bag to Malcolm, and he cautiously looked inside. "All *right*; I'll take the chicken. Is fish all right for you, Cora?"

Cora tore off her respirator, and was still rather on the perturbed side. "Wait a minute! Wait just *one minute*! This stuff could be poisoned or something! Shouldn't we test it?"

Malcolm was already digging into the chicken. "Ok, I'm testing it..." He continued talking through a mouthful of chicken. "Yep, it tastes good. Ok if we split the cookies?"

17

Telephones were ringing off the hook (so to speak) at the various mobile phone companies, as well as the government agencies that regulated that particular industry. The phone stoppage and Biepal message phenomena were worldwide. Everyone was asking about Biepal, and wanted to know why anyone would be trying to stop or regulate it, especially if it interfered with their texts, viewing of inane videos, or other vital functions of modern existence.

Much to his dislike, General Dithering was once again back in the Oval Office, answering to the President of the United States. "Mr. President sir, and I have to be honest here, we really have no idea how the nefarious party or parties involved in this clear act of mobile phone terrorism executed this phone stoppage, or sent that message. We can't seem to trace it anywhere; it just appeared out of nowhere. From what we can tell, it entered every tower related to cell phone reception, everywhere in the world, all at the same time."

President Hemminhough was wearing his most determined look, as taught to him by his marketing people, and perfected after several grueling hours in front of a mirror. "Well, Dithering, that ridiculous FDA idea of yours didn't work very well, did it? I told you it was a bad idea, but nobody listens to me! After all, I'm *just* the President! Get back with those FDA people, and call off this restriction business. And make sure they announce it loud and clear; the mobile phone companies are some of my biggest contributors!"

Dithering departed the Oval Office, looking rather dejected. His next call was to Marjorie Tapparatchnik, the FDA Commissioner.

Approximately 1.384 weeks later, Farpel had dropped in to the Hensworthy residence to pick up his carrots, and found yet another holo-message waiting for him. He returned to their living room the next afternoon. They were expecting him, with GadgiYacks properly nostril-ized.

"Why, Mr. Farpel, lovely to see you, as always."

"Yea, lady, nice to see you, too. I received your holo-message in my carrot box. I suppose you want to know about that little trick with those communicator gadgets of yours."

Mrs. Hensworthy looked knowingly at Malthorp. "Well, Malthorp and I were quite curious as to how you brought it about."

Malthorp chimed in. "Yes, Mr. Farpel, you do have a certain, shall we say, extraordinary ability when it comes to convincing people to see your point of view."

"Yea, well, it's not too much of a challenge when you have good Kinglorfs and equipment. We kinda use these bio-neural intelligent processors, or BIPs, as we call'em, for my gambling places, to evaluate crowd behavior, and make sure the patrons win just enough to keep coming back. But BIPs are real, *real* flexible in what they can do, so I just sorta redirected some BIPs to track signals in a certain frequency range on this rock you call home, and used *that* data to sort out the location of every tower involved in what you call 'cellular reception.' Then I applied some more BIPs to establish a temporary, fully enveloping interdimensional micro-rift in the vicinity of each tower, so that the signals associated with the cell towers disappeared into an adjacent dimension for a period of what you guys interpret as 'one hour.' I had a pretty good idea that no one here would figure out my strategy, given you guys are kinda limited to this single 3-space of yours. I don't know how you live this way; I'd find it pretty claustrophobic."

"*Anyway*, I used the same BIPs to send my own signal to each tower, with my little 'love note' about Biepal. My hench-Kinglorfs used the GadgiYack tech to make sure the messages were all in the right language for their locale. And *WOINK*, there you go. Message received."

Mrs. Hensworthy just shook her head in awe. "I must say, Mr. Farpel, that interdimensional capability of yours does come in handy."

"Best thing I ever learned in school, lady. I need to get going now; I heard about some action or other on the Whoola Planets, and I kinda need to check it out, so I can be sure that we can keep up with the Biepal demand. I'll be back for the next box of carrots." With that, Farpel rose to the ceiling, and disappeared once again as the interdimensional rift closed behind him.

About 24.226 days later, Farpel dropped in on the Hensworthys to pick up his most recent box of carrots, and wasn't looking particularly happy, for a Kinglorf. The Hensworthys were concerned.

"Well, Barnorklets, we have a bit of a problem."

A moment later, and before Farpel could continue, a small dot appeared in the middle of the Hensworthy's living room bookcase, and slowly grew to a reasonably sized interdimensional opening. Brobding Measelfort proceeded to step through.

Mrs. Hensworthy smiled broadly. "Why, Mr. Measelfort! It has been some time! How have you been? It's so lovely to see your multi-legged form again."

Brobding worked his way through the interdimensional rift he had formed in the transdimensional transport tube wall that passed nearest to the Hensworthy living room, but he had made the opening a little too small this time. He continued to squeeze through. "Greetings, Hensworthys! Excuse me while I... extricate myself... from this... opening!" Brobding finally popped through the rift, and achieved full living room status. "There, that's better! Yes, Mrs. Hensworthy, it has been too long! Our friend Farpel here left me a hollow-message, asking me to join you all for a little chat, so here I am!"

"Well, your timing is excellent, Mr. Measelfort; from what I just heard, Mr. Farpel was about to tell us about a little problem. Please continue, Mr. Farpel."

Farpel just looked around the room for a long moment. "Are we good now? Everyone comfy? Hey, Meas, welcome aboard. Now as I was *saying*, we have a problem, or, to be more accurate, are about to have a problem, with the Biepal supply."

Everyone took a moment to consider what Farpel had just brought to the proverbial table. Malthorp was the first to react. "Is there some issue with the biepalfruit, Mr. Farpel?"

"Funny you should say that, because that's exactly the issue. The Whoola Planets are entering their warm period, and apparently the biepalfruit shrubs are going dormant. No biepalfruit, no Biepal."

A little background might be useful here. Whoolagans (which would be how one refers to the residents of the Whoola Planets) have kept weather and planetary behavioral records for millennia. It turns out that the Whoola Planets have an interesting long-term weather cycle of approximately 47,382 planetary revolutions (that would be for Whoola 4a; Whoola 4b has a similar weather cycle of 48,224 revolutions, but let's not get picky here). The cycles are based on the planets' varying distances from the Whoola Star over time, due to a fairly complex orbital path.

At a certain point in this cycle, the Whoola Planets both slowly approach their perihelion, when they're closest to the Whoola Star. As a result, they tend to have a drier climate for approximately 1,496 planetary revolutions.

Because their orbital cycles are of slightly different lengths, a visitor seeking the particularly humid conditions generally found on these planets can satisfy his, her or its needs with one planet or the other for most of the time. There is a period of approximately 153 planetary revolutions, however, when both planets are simultaneously much drier than usual.

Whoolagans make it a point to enjoy more frequent beach vacations during these periods; the most humid areas of Wowserlik 3, the beach planet, are a popular alternative, particularly those areas where a rain forest resides just behind a small strip of sandy shoreline.

A more serious matter, however, at least from our perspective, involves the production of biepalfruit. During the warmest of this 153-Whoola-year period, the biepalfruit shrubs enter a sort of hibernation, preserving their moisture content, with a vast decrease in fruit production. Unfortunately for Farpel, Brobding Measelfort, and the Hensworthys, the Whoola Planets had just fully entered such a period, and the squeezing of the biepalfruit had come to a virtual standstill.

As a result, supplies of Biepal dried up, so to speak, dramatically. Any Biepal that remained was allocated, in accordance with a long-standing informal agreement among the local galactic beings, to those planets having inhabitants with the most appendages. Therefore, Bladger 3 received the largest share, as the Bladgerians were fairly friendly, fuzzy quadringentipedes, each sporting four hundred legs. (It's worth noting that shoe salespeople do extraordinarily well on Bladger 3.) Whenever a Bladgerian actually thought about walking with all those appendages, its legs would become hopelessly confused. The poor Bladgerian would then end up sitting in one spot, generally at or near a dining locale, feeling somewhat depressed. Given the combination of its location and demeanor, it would often overindulge in the cuisine; particularly the desserts. This made for some seriously overweight Bladgerians. And a chubby quadringentipede is no laughing matter.

By imbibing a flagon of Biepal with the meal, the Bladgerian mind tended to wander elsewhere; of course, their minds didn't actually wander off and leave their bodies, unlike the minds of the Vanator Snails of LeChien 4, whose brains had little legs of their own that allowed them to wander from shell to shell. In any case, when the Bladgerian mind was appropriately distracted, its legs were able to function autonomously in a far better fashion, without all that extra thinking going on. But let's get back to our story.

The gathering took a few moments in silence to consider the ramifications of a Biepal shortage. Malthorp had a thought. "Tell me, Mr. Farpel, do you have any supplies warehoused, by any chance? Perhaps we can continue with that for the time being."

Farpel nodded in the negative, and didn't look any happier. "One more shipment. That's it. After that, it's whatever you beings have on hand on this particular planet."

Everyone looked a little sad at the news, but Brobding Measelfort lightened the mood in short order. "Well, we did very well with the supplies you managed to secure, Farpel! And Hensworthys, you did an excellent job arranging for the product distribution. We should celebrate our success! And I'm sure we can come up with another good idea."

Farpel nodded in agreement. "Meas is right. We managed to get a goodly amount of Biepal sold on this little rock you beings call home, and avoid all the crazies here who tried to get in our way. And with all those carrots, I'm pretty satisfied with the take. Meas, are you satisfied with your share? Hensworthys?"

The other parties all nodded in agreement. Mrs. Hensworthy looked at Malthorp as she spoke. "Mr. Farpel, I believe Malthorp and I are *most* satisfied with the income provided by our little Biepal venture."

Malthorp smiled. "Well, I know one person who'll be happy to see Biepal disappear. This should put a big smile on Colonel Messington's sour countenance."

The attendees continued chatting briefly before the extraterrestrial members of the party returned through their respective interdimensional portals. Mrs. Hensworthy agreed to contact the distributor, and let them know that the supply of Biepal would soon be coming to an end.

Several Earth weeks later, word had gotten back to the various authorities investigating the 'Biepal situation' that Biepal would soon be disappearing from the shelves of the various shops that had it on offer. At about the same time, the Hensworthys were enjoying a quiet afternoon at home when there was a knock upon their door. Malthorp went to investigate, and, much to his surprise, Malcolm Schlectwetter, one of their favorite spies, was standing outside. "May I help you?"

Malcolm looked a little nervous. "Hi, I've been in the vacuum cleaner repair truck with my partner Cora. But I think you kind of knew that."

Malthorp nodded knowingly, and Malcolm continued.

"Well, I just wanted to let you know that we really appreciated the dinner a few weeks ago, and we'll be moving on to another assignment. Apparently, there's a French bakery called Bordeau Brioche that's frequented by our boss Colonel Messington. He said they've been making kind of doughy croissants lately, and as a result, he thinks it might be some kind of front, so we'll be observing them for a while." Just then, he noticed his spy partner Cora Nosely poking around the corner of the truck's back door, waving and, as usual, looking annoyed; Malcolm figured he better wrap up. "Anyway, it was nice spying on you."

Malthorp wasn't sure how to respond to this, but he tried a friendly smile. "Well, thank you for letting us know, and do enjoy your next assignment." With that, Malcolm ran hurriedly back to the truck as Malthorp closed the door.

Sergeant Major DeLade Greene was in Colonel Messington's office when the Biepal news arrived. "And there you have it, sir, there indeed! I told you I would get this Biepal business resolved, and there you go, all nice and neat and tidy. We'll have no more of that! No, no, no! Of that, I can most certainly assure you!"

Colonel Messington just looked at Greene as he spoke. "Oh, do shut up Greene, won't you?! I'm just glad to have this whole affair behind us! And hopefully we won't hear any more of this Taller versus Shorter business."

On the subject of Tallers versus Shorters, Extrilax Pharmaceuticals was continuing in its efforts to perfect a Biepal vaccine that would return Tallers to their original height, even as the distributor announced the eventual disappearance of the beverage. Extrilax scientists were persisting with their long-term clinical trials when they observed the most extraordinary result.

As I'm sure you recall, Extrilax was testing two vaccine variations. With Variation A, participants quickly shrank; they were seen to be 2.5 to 3 feet tall within six weeks of initiating treatment. With Variation B, subjects developed a fairly remarkable coating of long purple fur all over the bodies, though they tended to shed in the summertime.

And these weren't even the extraordinary parts. No, something even more remarkable had occurred.

Keep in mind that the trial participants hadn't indulged in Biepal since the beginning of the trials. Several weeks after the Biepal announcement, or approximately 1.382 years since the beginning of the trial, the *placebo groups* for both vaccine variations, as well as the actual Variation B vaccine recipients, began shrinking! The scientists involved had no good explanation for this.

When asked about the contents of the placebo vaccines, Dr. Sabrina Schmerzen, one of the lead trial scientists, explained, "Why, it's nothing more than saline, with a proprietary additive that provides a little extra pain at the injection site. After all, we wanted the placebo to match as closely as possible to the vaccine being tested.   I can't understand how those participants are now *shrinking*, but if it works, it works!" When asked about the direction of the research in light of these new results, Dr. Schmerzen indicated that a new *Variation C* vaccine, predicated on the placebo contents, would now be developed and placed in the Extrilax sales pipeline.

Unfortunately, the Variation A recipients retained their seriously diminished stature, and the Variation B recipients continued to contend seasonally with purple fur. Well, nobody's perfect.

About one month later, an article published in *The Chicago Journal of Inexpensive Medical Solutions* postulated that perhaps the height effects of Biepal simply wore off over time. The article was quickly discounted by the medical profession, however, with experts pointing out that the authors had failed to conduct a large, well-funded, industry-supported double-blind clinical trial to arrive at their conclusion.

The seasons were changing, the leaves upon the deciduous trees were offering their extraordinary autumnal colors in Earth's northern hemisphere, and the world had more or less returned to normal.

As for Biepal, several notable basketball teams, who shall remain nameless, were purportedly hoarding some of the last known bottles for their own special purposes. And if one really searched for it, the lucky consumer might find a dusty bottle in the back storeroom of certain random establishments that stock such wares.

By the way, tall people have become rather annoyed at being asked whether they indulged in Biepal, so we don't recommend asking them; unless, of course, you know them quite well.

The Hensworthys thought often about their Biepal experience. They enjoyed the occasional visit from their good friend Brobding Measelfort, who always relished a nice cup of tea in the general vicinity of the Hensworthy's fireplace.

On one such visit, the subject of Farpel came up once again. Mrs. Hensworthy looked pensive as she sipped her tea. "He certainly did enjoy those boxes of carrots." The others nodded in agreement. After a brief and quiet interlude, Brobding Measelfort spoke up.

"You know, I have an interesting idea."

Stay tuned for the next exciting adventure!...

B